BOOK 1

PROJECT CHRONOS
THE WAR BEGINS

BOOK 1

PROJECT CHRONOS
THE WAR BEGINS

STEVE ANTONETTE

Primix Publishing
11620 Wilshire Blvd
Suite 900, West Wilshire Center, Los Angeles, CA, 90025
www.primixpublishing.com
Phone: 1 (888) 585-7476

Published by Primix Publishing   02/17/2021

ISBN: 978-1-954886-00-1(sc)
ISBN: 978-1-954886-01-8(e)

Library of Congress Control Number: 2021902646

Contents

Acknowledgements

This is for my family and friends, for your years of support, encouragement and finding the time to get together for a coffee and allowing me to bounce my crazy ideas off of you, it really does help me think and create. Thank you for your fun zany input, hopefully some of you will notice I tried to reconstruct some of those thoughts into this story.

This book would never be if it wasn't for all of you.

Supers: The Chameleon

Almost one year ago from today:

Nick was a man with a unique set of espionage skills and had an array of gizmos and gadgets to compliment them. Most notable was his suit. The camouflage technology built into the suit could automatically match whatever color surrounded it, as long as he remained relatively still. He also possessed high-tech goggles that can switch between night vision, infrared, or thermo with a subtle turn of the dial: everything a cat-burglar needed to infiltrate the premises.

He was well-known too, claiming he could sneak into any location without detection because he blended his way in and slithered on out. That's how he adopted the nickname, The Chameleon.

He stalked the seven-story building from the bush line, using his night vision to observe the patrol patterns and spot any potential surveillance cameras.

With the guard's scarce, the cameras diverted, this was his moment he'd been waiting for. With haste he bolted across the grass and, as he approached the wall of the building, he aimed with his air-powered grapple gun. Once it fastened to the roof, the wire retracted and carried him all the way up.

The roof wasn't well guarded, giving Nick plenty of time to cut his way into the mainframe wires, plug in his handheld computer and begin scanning through the company's files. It only took a few minutes for the device to search through countless personal files and technical schematics, before he found the data he came for.

He was hacking into a company known as Chronos, a covert government branch that used Supers as mercenaries for unique missions that required extraordinary beings. Nick had heard a rumor that the CEO used the resources to hunt down fellow Supers and bring them in for experimental testing.

Nick was hacking the world-renown procedure and research that apparently granted Normals' super abilities. It wasn't successful to date and had taken hundreds of lives before it was officially banned a few months back by the government. They ordered it to be erased and the equipment destroyed. Whoever still possessed the data would be sentenced to prison and brought up on charges.

Nick himself was only a Normal, so sure, there was a time even he was tempted to take the procedure. But the zero success rate is what stopped him and most. Even if he changed his mind, he couldn't now anyway.

Nick didn't want it, his client did and for whatever reason didn't matter, as long as he got paid. Maybe his client wanted to prefect the procedure to begin his own experiments or sell it on the black market, it didn't matter to Nick, only money did.

Once the download reached roughly halfway, the failsafe alarm triggered; alerting everyone on the premise of Nick's presence.

But Nick didn't worry, after all this wasn't the first time he's been in this type of predicament. He figured he had a few moments before the low paid security guards were on to him. But just in case, he stayed on the ready and patiently waited for the data to finish downloading.

Just as it was about to finish, a gust of wind brushed past, like something or one remarkably fast whizzed by. Nick suddenly found out he was no longer alone when the mystery figure standing behind him coughed out.

"What are you doing up here stranger?" Startled, Nick turned to see who he now shared the lonely rooftop with. Staring back was a clean-shaven man with long slicked blonde hair, dressed in a black suit. Covering his face was a pair of sunglasses with a band instead of arms; presumably to keep the glasses from blowing off when he moved incredibly fast.

Nick stood tall and cracked a smile. He was no stranger to the man across from him. "Hey Bryan, I was curious who they'd send up."

The fast man smirked back. "Well, I am the fastest. The others will be here shortly, I wouldn't worry. Now," He slowly inched forward. "Hand over the device and I'll go easy on you."

Nick noticed the download finally finished. He retrieved the device with one hand while the other reached into his pocket. "I don't think you're that fast Bryan…" And with that, he pulled out a smoke bomb and tossed it towards Bryan's feet.

But Bryan was and proved it by snatching the bomb in midair, run across the roof, toss it over the ledge, and ran back before Nick could even turn around. "Why does everyone doubt my speed?" Bryan commented as he grabbed the thief by the wrist, and removed the goggles. "Now don't make me force it from you."

Nick found out besides being fast, Bryan was also quite strong and couldn't shake free. He replied. "Come on, I can't let it go that easily." With a slight flick of his free wrist, out shot a small blade that pierced through the belly of his victim. Nick helped his attacker gently fall to the ground and whispered. "Sorry old friend, but we both know, you'll be fine."

Knowing more will be arriving at any moment, Nick raced towards the edge and courageously leaped off. He stuck out his arms from his body to span the wings and glided high into the night sky. The suit matched the black sky to conceal his escape as others finally arrived to Bryan's aid.

Just as Nick thought he had escaped, from high above, a hulking humanoid bat tackled him in midair, and together, both collided to the ground.

The eight-foot-tall bat lifted the sore thief by the throat so they were face to face. The bat wasn't much for words, it just snarled and continued to squeeze on his victim's larynx. It managed to crush the suit, wrecking the camouflage technology, returning it to a solid grey color.

Right as Nick was about to pass out, a slender female appeared from out of nowhere and spoke to the bat. "That's enough Superbat, Peterson wants him alive."

The hulking monster obliged the woman and released his chokehold. As Nick gasped for some air, she took him by the arm, and with a blink of an eye, the two of them vanished.

When Nick came to, he found himself strapped to a cold metal lab table surrounded by frantic scientists preparing for an operation. As his senses became clear, he heard someone barking orders and tilted his head to the familiar face.

Once he saw that Nick was finally awake, he smiled. He was standing at the foot of the table, exhaling the fumes of his cigar. This man needed no introduction. The CEO of Chronos tried to give Normals what every Super took for granted.

He's been around for decades, worked with many Supers, and helped the government with impossible tasks too. Rumors began to spread that he was ageless, he looked like a man in his late forties, but he's always looked that way.

He had a deep tone and talked like a man who's seen it all. "Ah, the famous Chameleon; I must commend you, not everyone could sneak into my premise and hack into my files." He noticed Nick paid more attention to the scientists who were placing syringes into various spots of his body.

With a confident grin, he continued. "If you wanted to volunteer yourself and help me figure out where we went wrong, all you had to do was ask."

"I don't want it, I wasn't…" Nick didn't want to give up his source. At least he finally figured out what they were prepping him for. "It doesn't work, and the survival rate is like two percent."

"Relax Nick, do I look worried? You see, my scientists have finally discovered the solution. Well, we hope anyway. Are you familiar with the different blood types and strains that are out there? I rather not bore you or repeat what I had to suffer through. You'll just have to put faith into this. Doctor Wells' team here is going to inject you with blood from a select group of Supers and see if he is right. Again, thanks for volunteering."

Even though there was no point, Nick struggled. He asked. "Why don't you just interrogate me like you normally do?"

Peterson blew the cigar smoke into the captured man's face. With a smug grin, he remarked. "Why bother, you never talk. Well, never anything useful comes out of that yap of yours." Peterson gave the go-ahead nod to his scientists. As he walked away he made one final comment. "Oh, I must warn you; this procedure can be incredibly painful. Usually, we induce our patients with some sedatives to help cope. But a tough guy like you, I see no need. You like pain…"

Nick was groggy as he woke up in his cell bed. He sat up, rubbed his eyes, and tried to recall what happened. He went over to use the facet to splash some cold water on his face. When he looked up to see himself in the mirror, he saw only the wall that was behind him. Startled that he had no reflection, he staggered back. Pressing up against the wall, he looked down and was able to still see his hands and feet. But when he stared back through the mirror, he wasn't there.

Completely befuddled he asked. "What did they do to me?"

While trying to piece what happened together, the nearby guard came by to do his routine inspection and saw the empty cell.

In a panic, he called for backup as he unlocked the cell. The guard rushed towards the bed and flipped it over.

Nick remained quiet and still, questioning why he could see himself but the guard couldn't. He slowly sidestepped to the door, exited, and locked the cage, trapping the guard inside.

Leaving the guard to figure it out on his own, Nick made a fast dash down the hallway before this new and useful ability wore off.

Watching the confused Chameleon make his invisible and easy escape through the surveillance monitors from an unknown office was Mister Peterson. By his side stood Bryan the speedster fidgeting with his fingers. Standing proud was Doctor Wells, looking rather pleased with his results.

Peterson commented. "So, it would seem we finally have a success. I guess you were right Doctor, we needed her blood." Peterson couldn't contain his overwhelming joy any further. He then excitedly asked. "So now we can move forward Doctor Wells?"

"That is correct sir, once we gather everything we need to continue." An ill-mannered Peterson slowly spun around so he could glare the good Doctor in the face.

Wells trembled with fear.

Peterson only wanted results at this point, not more problems.

Growing impatient, Peterson blew smoke into the doctor's face as he asked. "Well, what are we missing still?"

"Supers sir. We need the blood of Supers. If you want certain abilities, you'll need the blood of a pure Super with that particular ability to replicate it." The Doc adjusted his glasses and continued. "As you know, we currently only have access to a few and I know you want more. Not to mention, you want a Psychic. There is only one known Psychic out there and he'll be next to impossible to get."

"Yes, Venkman..." Peterson plotted as he sucked in some of that intoxicating cigar smoke. "Don't worry about him." He turned to the speedster Bryan, who was eager to do something. Standing in one spot wasn't something someone with his speed liked to do. " I want you to start collecting all Supers. Maybe we can find some more willing participants to aid us in this task."

"Isn't the government going to be wary of what you're doing? And I don't think Sue or the Bat will be gung-ho on this." Bryan asked.

Peterson thought over the pending problem and asked. "Do we still have that mole Agent Pongo sent in?"

"Yes sir, but we had to toss a mask on him and not allow anyone to speak to him. You know very well what he is capable of. He's almost escaped several times now."

With a crafty grin like he was recalling something from long ago, Peterson replied. "Ah yes, with his unique gifts, it would only be wise to use Kyle to act as my liaison. With his silver tongue, he can keep the government out of the way and those conflicted with morals on our path. Were you able to snatch his family?"

Bryan nodded. "With ease." He saw Nick finally get free from the building. "And what about him? You're not just going to let him go, are you? You gave him the perfect set of abilities to make him undetectable."

Peterson continued to monitor the screen and watch as the invisible man he couldn't see but know was there and escaping. "We need him to escape; I want to find out who he's going to run to."

Doctor Wells also added. "We're also going to need more blood from Miss Marik as well. Her blood combined with the Super whose ability you wish to have."

Bryan stated the obvious. "Her blood wasn't so easy to get the first time 'round. We're going to need some help to get close to her. Especially with her company at her beck and call."

Peterson chuckled as he inhaled more from his burning cigar. "It's ironic; I worked alongside her for many years, plotting my little secret agenda. Spent many long nights trying to figure out why it wasn't working. Meanwhile, the answer is literally right next to me."

Wells went to explain by Peterson didn't want to attend a science lesson. He cut in with a stern tone. "Just find me more guinea pigs to experiment on. I still have unanswered questions that need addressing before I proceed on myself..."

SUPERS: THE JUNKER

Six months ago from today:

The crowd was on their feet raising the roof of the stadium. The results of one heck of an underdog matchup between the lightweight Champion and the Heavyweight Champion of the MMA.

The fighters stood with their team in their respective corners as the ring announcer stood in the middle of the ring to declare the winner of the event. "Winner of this unsanctioned David versus Goliath matchup, Stacey Malone!"

A man, standing about six feet tall, very athletic build, with long black curly hair and unshaven face took the middle of the octagon and started blowing kisses at the ladies in the audience and flexing his muscles to intimidate their spouses. He was arrogant and full of confidence as he took both championship belts and held them high over his head.

Then a reporter stuck a microphone in his face and asked, "Malone, you've done practically everything now. Your rookie years in hockey, baseball, football, boxing, the list goes on, but each one, you manage to bring home the championships. How do you do it?"

He had those rugged looks, and with that smirk, he boasted. "Well, yours truly is just that damn good Princess. If you'd like a private session with Champ and see how he does his workout regime, he's sure you two can figure something out." He gave her a poise wink.

Considering this man just went through ten rounds with someone easily forty pounds of muscle bigger, he appeared healthy and unscathed.

Before she gave him an answer, the Champ, along with his team and his new prize belts, headed for the locker room.

Later that evening when it was just Stacey and his manager in his loft. What a man cave, sports posters, and random paraphernalia scattered all around. Dirty clothes blanketed the rooms and his sweaty smelly gear made nice decorations throughout the place. Stacey was sitting on his old favorite rocker that he got from his Grandpa and was cringing over the sports highlights.

A troubled Frank finally broke the silence. "Ok, Stace, seriously now, when are we going to talk about this? I thought we had agreed..."

The Champ looked somewhat confused. "Talk about what, we always watch the highlights."

"No, about this sudden change of yours. You said you weren't going to take that super drug. It wasn't successful yet and killed more..."

The Champ chuckled. "Come on Frankie, you know the Champ says no to drugs. Besides, it was banned remember?"

"If you didn't take it, then there's got to be something wrong..."

"Wrong?" He continued to laugh. "You're kidding right, Frank? I've never felt better, look at me." He didn't have a scratch on him. "That guy should have owned me, but thankfully yours truly decided to carry him through eight rounds so the fans didn't feel cheated." He then went back to watching the highlights because he had a side bet on the match and wanted to make sure he was winning.

"Listen, I'm just saying don›t keep these stunts up. If I›m asking them, you›ll be sure the Press will be. And then what? What will you tell them?»

Stacey shrugged. "That I possess great skills due to great training?"

"You know the Press will blow this out of whack right. If they figure out you're some Super using your abilities for greed. I think of you like a son Stace, please be careful. You know what happens to Supers. I think you should perhaps do some good..."

Stacey jumped out off the couch in a heat of rage. "What, just because I got these abilities, I owe the world something? Come on, I'm just a pro-athlete Frank. I'm no hero. Heck, I'm just enjoying life, you should be too."

Frank tried to get him to see the bigger picture. "Some things are more important than money and fame. One day, you'll see that. Lots of crime and slime out there infecting our streets and nobody is doing anything about it. But you could."

Stacey felt the spark. The thought that he could beat people up for fun caught his attention. "What do you want me to do huh? Toss a mask, get out there, and stop crime? What if I get shot?"

"What if you make a difference? But you're damn tough, did you see that guy tonight? I bet you're practically bulletproof." Frankie knew how to goad and persuade the Champ into doing things he didn't necessarily want to do at the time

Feeling quite invincible now, Stacey gave it some serious thought. "It did feel good laying the beat down on that chump. And I could make a difference..."

"I think you'll be amazing. At least try it for a night. See what can happen?"

Now onboard, Stacey began rubbing his stubble to think. "Alright Frankie, I'll do it. But won't I need a costume or something? We don't need someone recognizing the Champ."

"Oh, what, you don't want that free publicity? You thrive on attention, what gives now?"

Stacey gave him that, are you serious look. "Hey, we don't need people thinking their Champ is a mutant monster; think of the kids, their hero, a Super. We both know the reputation Supers have. Not a good one and if we want to keep getting these sweet gigs and making money, we better stay on the down-low."

"Ok, what kind of gimmick you want?" Frank was thinking of an idea for his costume as he panned the loft. "Why don't you just toss on some old sports gear; the extra padding wouldn't hurt."

Stacey chuckled, "And what, toss on a hockey mask? I think that figure has already been done."

"Exactly, already a rep out there for him, a psycho, you could use that to your advantage."

"What about weapons?" The Champ got to thinking, he was appearing to like this idea the more and more they discussed it.

Frank kicked over some of the sports equipment just lying around. Dozens of wooden bats and sticks were sticking out from under the couch. "Keep up that façade. It's not like you're using them anyway."

Stacey continued to rub his chin, it helped him think. "Sure, I'll just toss them in a golf bag. How's this guy supposed to get around?"

"You got your bike. Use that."

"We can't have this guy riding around on the Champ's motorcycle. How would that look?"

"You got a knack for picking up stuff quick. Give that parkour crap a go; you know, street-running. Just jump from one rooftop to the other." Frankie collected some of the old gear from the corner and started tossing it over at the Champ. "Get some of that on, see how you look."

"Going to need a name, something for those petty punks to fear and remember me by." Stacey started to gear up. Some of it worked, but most didn't. The ones that didn't get discarded back to the corner. "Got to be something that strikes fear but easy for those JV low-lives to remember."

Both were now getting right into this whole vigilante feel, They began treating it like a fight. "Don't forget to trash talk and be downright cocky. Let 'em think you're out there!"

"Yeah, the mind games. Get the smack talk in. I'm digging this now Frankie."

"That's great! Time to get out there and clean the junk up off the streets!"

It suddenly hit Stacey. "I like it Frank, Junk, the Junker. It's got two meanings. First the obvious, but more importantly, it speaks for my massive junk; give the damsels I save something to think about." He then let loose a playful wink all while his old pal Frankie shook his head in a mock shame.

The night sky was clear, the moonlight lit up the dark seedy alleys of the neighborhood. The Junker just made another successful land on a rooftop and took a moment to peer down. The cries of a frightened young girl could be heard from a block away. She was being chased down by several petty thugs looking for a good time. Bruised and cut, she ran for her life. Then suddenly her heel broke, twisted her ankle that caused her to trip and fall hard on her face.

The gang had no trouble catching up to her as the lead one pounced on top. "Hey Baby, where you going? We were just startin' to have fun."

"Please, don't, I beg you…" She used all her might to fend him off but it wasn't enough.

The remaining punks circled; eagerly waiting for their turn to come.

Stacey had seen enough and leaped down. Using a deep gritty tone, he said. "Penalty, too many douche-bags on the ice."

That grabbed their attention and in unison, turned to see who would be dumb enough to interrupt their fun. And they got to see who indeed. Standing there before them, in a commanding and intimidating stance was the Champ dressed up his collected sports gear and wielding his well-used hockey stick.

The one youngster chuckled and remarked. "Who's this joker?"

Another teen turned to his friend rather confused and asked. "Hey man, am I hallucinating or does that dude looked awfully like that crazy hockey guy from…"

Stacey cut in. "Listen you pathetic punks, I'm the Junker and you're the junk. And it's trash day!"

Each thug then pulled out various weapons that they had on them. One with a lead pipe, one a blade, and another had a baton. The three charged the Junker, who had no trouble sidestepping and using the stick to take them out. While busy rendering each thug unconscious, the lead teen stood up, removed a revolver from his waistline, and took aim.

Before the victim could shout out, the teen squeezed the trigger and the bullet shot out. It struck Stacey in the chest and it bounced off but left one nasty welt behind. It hurt, but Stacey kept his game face on. That left each thug frozen and wide-eyed. None wanted to mess with him and they all dropped their weapons and scurried off.

Feeling quite satisfied with his first successful rescue, the Junker put his weapon away and helped the distressed girl to her feet. After a much deserving hug of her gratitude, she thanked him. The Junker decided to take full advantage of the situation. He made sure he had a firm grip of all her posteriors and the appalled look she gave didn't seem to faze him.

"No problemo toots." The Champ continued to boast. "Make sure you tell your hot friends that there's a new player in town. I'm the Junker, here to clean up these infested streets."

The next morning came; Stacey was passed out on the couch, exhausted from the long night of patrolling the streets and beating up thugs.

Frank stormed into his loft and immediately turned the TV on. "Stace, check it out man, you made the morning news!"

He rolled over as Frank turned up the volume. A reporter was interviewing the girl he saved that night. She was making her closing statement. "Well, you heard it right guys. There are Supers out there helping us Normals after all. Will more like him join his side, or will they continue to be greedy and seek out their agendas? Today a petition was started. People are asking the city to start a Super Hero group to keep us safe. I don't know about you, but I have already signed my name, being the one-hundredth to do so this morning. If this goes through, I know I'll be able to sleep soundly at night."

Frank patted his pal on the back. "Wow Stace, you really started something here. See, I told you that you'd be a hit."

The Champ sat up and reached for his empty bottle of whiskey. "Was there any doubt? I'm loveable. I have to be honest Frankie, I did some serious thinking. And you're absolutely right, these times are rough, it's only going to get worse before it gets better. And people like yours truly need to step up. Not just for the Normal folks, but others like me. We can't be afraid to come out, even with those SBU punks hunting us down. We need to show them that not all of us are bad, and who better than this perfectly sexy specimen that stands before you?"

Stacey went down to city hall, where thousands of people had already gathered to hear the response from the Mayor on his answer to this pending petition. Stacey had his mind already set on speaking up and announcing that he was the Junker and that he will be the first to sign up for the City's Hero group.

As the Mayor stepped to the microphone, another vigilante hopped onto the platform. He opened his mouth to speak- and three darts slammed into his chest in quick succession. He collapsed to the ground. Agents rushed forward to bind the unconscious Super before he could wake.

Stacey scanned the nearby rooftops and spotted the SBU snipers who had taken the man down. "Well so much for signing up," he muttered under his breath.

The Mayor continued. "We understand your concerns and I have taken this petition into account. But we already have a division in place to police these Supers and to protect us Normals. The SBU has been doing a superb job for many years now. These vigilantes like this uprising Junker fellow are only hindering the solution. Believe me, they are not helping. We have now issued a Super registration act, if you have any unique ability; you must report yourself to the SBU headquarters and be taken to the island. There they'll asset you and declare if you are fit to come back to live with us or be kept there."

With the people chanting out "boos" and some cheering, another man in a black suit, sunglasses stepped in. "Morning folks, I'm SBU agent Eric Pongo, head of the Super department. Please, understand, with these sudden outbursts by these Supers, we're not saying you're all hostile. We just need to make sure. If you volunteer and come in without trouble, it will definitely go towards you in our decision to allow you to return."

The Champ shook his head; he knew a lie when he saw one. It was part of his new abilities; he could just read someone and know if they were lying. "Well, what does one do now?"

Suddenly from above the podium, an athletically built man with slicked-back blonde hair slowly floated down and landed beside Agent Pongo. He wasn't wearing anything special, just an unbuttoned shirt with a plain black T-shirt underneath and black jeans. He went to introduce himself but paused like he sensed something bad was about to ensue. He held his hands out front of him and out of nowhere, a faint see-through force field erected and within mere seconds, a half-dozen darts struck the field and harmlessly bounced off.

Pongo quickly drew his service weapon and was about to take action but the mystery man turned to him, gazed into his eyes, and in a soft gentle voice said. "You don't want to shoot me."

Pongo, lowering his weapon repeated the words in a robotic monotone like he was being hypnotized. The mystery man then approached the Mayor and spoke more casually and addressed his concern. "Mister Mayor, I feel your decision today is going to hurt the Super community. And I urge you to change your mind. Today I declare, that I, Venkman, will willingly join and lead this Hero group." The crowd broke into a cheer; they liked what they saw. Most of them thought this was all a publicity act and a great lead up to starting a Super Hero Group.

Rather impressed, Stacey rubbed his unshaven face. This was impressive in itself, after all, it was hard to gain this world-renowned Champion's respect. "The Champ digs this guy's style and he seems rather powerful; someone the Champ should definitely consider joining."

Once Pongo was out of his daze, he joined the Mayor's side; who was quickly thinking over this man's proposal. Pongo spoke into the Mayor's ear. "Sir, are you seriously considering this man's offer?"

The Mayor motioned towards the people. "Do you hear them chanting for him? He has them on his side. Besides, I thought this was what you wanted, Supers exposing themselves and stepping out from the shadows?"

Pongo nodded, "Yeah I did. But do you know who this man is? Venkman is the twin brother of the notorious Maverine. He's a known psionic sir; he's most likely manipulating us this very minute."

'And reading your thoughts, but trust me please, I'm not using my mind-controlling powers at this moment. I have no need. I am related to Maverine, and for the record, no, he isn't as bad as he's made out to be.'

Alarmed, Pongo spun around to face Venkman, who was happily waving at the crowd, further boosting his influence. Meanwhile, SBU snipers repositioned themselves so they were now completely surrounding the podium. Malone spotted them first and ducked into a nearby alley to put on his disguise. Then, he leaped up the fire escape, gaining access to the roof.

With a pair of non-matching ball bats in his hands, he snuck up behind the snipers on this roof. "Hey, nobody likes the peanut gallery bubs." As they turned around in surprise, he swung the bats and knocked them out. Across the way, he saw another pair about to open fire. The Junker leaped down landed hard on the podium and rolled. As he somersaulted to his feet, he brought the bat up.

At the same time, the snipers fired, releasing the darts inside the barrel. Also at that same time, Venkman held out his left hand and erected another field, but one dart managed to get through but was stopped short when it imbedded into the wooden bat.

The cheers and whistles came to a sudden halt as they all stood there in awe and silence. With everyone's jaws hung low, Venkman's patience grew thin. He nodded to the Junker, silently thanking him, and turned back to both the Mayor and Pongo. "Tell your goons to stand down, or else."

Pongo wasn't willing to find out what the "or else" was from the most powerful Super known to man.

Venkman was good-hearted, but that didn't mean he was a pansy either. When it came down to it, he got his hands dirty.

The unwilling Pongo tapped on his earpiece and told the snipers to stand down. The look of hate and embarrassment filled his eyes. You knew he wasn't going to let this slide. One way or another, he will find a way to sack revenge; he just wasn't sure how or even when yet.

The mayor stuck out his hand and accepted Venkman as the first member of the City's Hero Squad and dubbed him their leader.

Venkman graciously accepted turned to the Junker and asked. "So, are you in…" He paused to hear not only his answer but his name.

The Junker nodded and gave the thumbs up. "Yeah, you can count the Junker in."

The name brought a smile to Venkman. "I like it, let's clean up the junk."

"That's the Junker's line bro."

SUPERS: MAVERINE

A few hours into the future:

A burly man in a trench coat impatiently sat on a bench in a hallway of a building that was half in ruins. Something obviously went wrong here. You could tell by the scorched walls, everything was drenched by the sprinkler system and missing sections of the exterior walls were blown away. But this hallway, the elevator down the hall, and the cafeteria around the corner were miraculously all intact.

The man was unshaven and wearing a pair of unusual looking high-tech goggles. It was a sunny afternoon; there was no need for them, but he did. At his feet, rested a hefty black duffle-bag full of dangerous artillery; from a massive .50 caliber, anti-tank rifle to handguns and even C-4 explosive; this bag was fully loaded. It had to weigh over a few hundred pounds, no normal human would even try to move it.

Many SBU agents were scouring about, searching for something and one. They were stacking computers together, files; basically, everything with information on it was going on a helicopter back to headquarters. Outside of the building, roughly a hundred armed agents had circled the perimeter and cut off all possible exits and waiting for the order to storm the building and apprehend the Super felon.

The female agent standing next to the Super tapped her ear, received her orders, and addressed the man. "Mister Maverine, Agent Greene is on her way, please be seated in the office."

The man gave her a slight nod as he stood up with the bag and headed for the office across the way. The office had been ransacked, the once smooth oak desk, torn oil painting on the far wall and grungy dark red plush carpet were things to notice as he entered. He walked through the burnt papers and scattered files to find the only available chair to have a seat and did his best to wait patiently.

Not even a minute had passed as a slender brunette female with a dark shadowy figure came into the room. The mystery guest did their best to keep his or her identity a secret as they remained in the corner to just listen in.

Agent Greene had quite the cheery smile and went to shake the hand of the impatient man. "Now Mister Mav…"

"Listen I keep telling you people, it's just Mav, or Maverine ok; none of this Mister crap."

"Ok," She sat down across from him. She was a tad nervous at first. After all, it wasn't every day a notorious Super, someone who is on the number one most dangerous list, sits across from you and you feel safe. But she kept her composure and conducted the meeting. "So, we both know why you're here; but we need to go over what happened exactly."

Mav himself was also quite uncomfortable. He didn't really know why he came. At the time he made this deal, he wasn't thinking. When you go by the seat of your pants planning, you don't rationalize things; you act on passion. But he was a man of his word.

"You want a debriefing on what happened? Do we have time for that? I could just write a report for you to skim through."

"There won't be a need for that. I am just the liaison in this matter. I'm here to make sure you know your rights and that this meeting is properly conducted to prevent legal infringements."

Maverine laughed when he replied. "Right? When did the SBU start caring about Supers and their rights?" Before she could respond, he continued. "I remember the SBU protocol and red tape they have to stick behind. It's the reason why people like me were hired by people like you back in the day. I'm just wondering why we're still sitting here. What do you people want from me?"

"Why don't you just start from the beginning?"

At first, he responded with a chuckle. But soon added. "From the beginning huh, that's going to take a while. I've seen a lot in my years, I don't know if we can cover all of it before we head to the island."

"I meant from the more recent activities. Why don't you just say why infamous cold-hearted Maverine got himself involved in all this?"

If she could see the glare he gave her through his goggles, she would wish she'd taken back what she just said. But he bit his tongue and spoke. "You know, in the old days, yeah I didn't mind the, he's a loose-cannon, stay out of his way, attitude people gave me. But come on, I'm trying to do right. Ok, I may go about it unorthodox; but it gets the job done."

"You were responsible for destroying this city and bringing it to smoldering ruins. How do you justify that?"

Maverine took a second to think over his answer. "Let's see, well it started when I got an email from Special SBU Agent Eric Pongo; he went into great detail with what Peterson was really up to.

Now we all know the SBU and the City's glory-seeking Heroes have a red tape you can't cross. As I said, I worked for you guys before, I know I got stuck with the shit missions that need to be off the books. And like before, here I am, getting the full blame. Hench why we're here."

Maverine let that sink in before finishing off with. "Chronos is a division of the SBU is it not? Your new Director didn't like working with Supers, he would rather spend time policing them and locking them up on some stupid island. But the government likes the idea. You guys need to work on your communication issues…"

Greene cut in. "Mister Maverine, please just stick to the facts of the events in question."

"The truth hurts, doesn't it? The facts are this, my friends started dying, I stepped in. Some guns went off, a few explosions…"

"Millions of dollars in damages and a city torn apart is hardly the result of a few explosions." But time was whittling away and he had information that she needed. She pressed for it. "So where do Venkman and the rest of his band of fame-seeking heroes fit into all this?"

Maverine didn't like that question. This meeting went from calm to heated with that question. "Never mind where they are. This is about me and my actions. That was the deal. I come voluntarily and you left them alone. You needed a patsy to pin this all on; that's me."

Greene was hesitant to reply and with the armed agents itching to storm in, Maverine grew impatient. He reached for his bag. "Listen, if you're going to break your end of the deal, then this is over and I'm leaving. You'll never see me or my friends again."

"Mister Maverine with all due respect here; the building is surrounded. You're not leaving here without answering our questions."

With a cold uncaring stare through those dark-tinted goggles, Mav remarked. "Is that supposed to be some kind of threat? Lady listen, I don't care how many agents you got ready to storm in, don't piss me off. And I know what you're thinking; they're armed with that negate serum crap that will shut my abilities down. Newsflash, if those crap darts somehow break through my tough skin, my healing has dealt with it before, which means it's built an antibody for it now. And that's assuming if any of your so-called skilled marksmen will manage to even hit me." He then stood up and prepared himself to leave. But he waited; to see if the agent would change her mind. "You can save many lives here Agent; it's all up to you."

She remained quiet as her rage was taking over. The mystery figure in the dark corner spoke up; he had a gritty tone like he was purposely masking his voice to not be recognized by the individual. "You're right, we did have an agreement. So please, as you were saying about what started all of this, take it from the start of the day."

As he planted himself back on the edge of the chair Mav began to explain the series of events that led up to the ultimate ending to the City of Supers. "Venkman and I had a plan set in motion. But I think it all began to go downhill when that new recruit started working for Chronos… What was his name? Mallaro, Mallarian… something like that. He started asking the wrong questions and screwing up missions; that rose suspicions and caught Peterson's attention…"

SUPERS: MALLARIAN

Now:

News broadcast:

A beautiful young brunette reporter was on the scene of a horrific destructive bank heist. The wall was in rubble, the vault door rested on a crushed police cruiser and SBU agents were containing the scene.

"We're here live at the First National Bank where witnesses claim that two Supers walked straight into the bank and stole all the money. An eye witness said and I quote; "the smaller robber shot electricity from his hands to take out the armed guards while the bigger brute marched to the vault and pried the door right off."

"Each day more and more Supers rise and not for the good. What will Mayor Strider and SBU Director Carey do about this Super problem?"

"Also who is this massive flying serpent roaming the skies at night? Friend or foe? Some claim that it devours other Supers. The City's fine Heroes sure have their work cut out for them."

"But today, things might change, because throughout the day, Miss Marik, one of the first Supers to publically announce herself and who started the shelter for others like her, will be meeting with the government officials, pleading them not to arm the police with the

SBU weapons. Does she have no sympathy for us Normals? Tune in tonight at six for more details as it concludes."

In the medium-sized well-furnished office of this massive seven-story building, hung a one-of-a-kind oil painting, and blanketing the floor was a dark-red plush carpet. The exterior windows were reinforced bulletproof glass and the walls were armored with half a foot of steel built right into the studs.

Sitting at his cluttered desk was a very charismatic yet, troubled looking man. He was quite striking to everyone who gazed their eyes upon him. At six-foot even, with blonde hair, blue eyes, and great physique, only helped him in his charisma.

Entering into his open-door office was another fellow around the same age, same height, build, but nowhere near as handsome. After he gently knocked, the man's troubles disappeared as he eagerly waved him in. The man standing was nervous and even stuttered when he asked. "Hey, there, Kyle, I'm here for..."

"Mister Mallarian," that smile could ease the angriest of men; his tone was deep, calm, and soothing to any ear listening. It was quite mesmerizing as well; even if you didn't agree with him, you felt compelled to do what was asked. Kyle didn't waste time to head over and shake the man's hand.

He had many files stacking tall on his desk and seemed to be scurrying about. "Our newest recruit, I see the procedure went smooth. Are you all up to speed?"

"Yes. Mr. Peterson said to come to see you; you can guide me around and help me acquaint myself with fellow personnel?"

"That I do, do. If you'll come with me, I have a lot of work that needs to get done. Today looks like it's going to be a real busy one." Kyle grabbed one of the many files scattered across his desk and escorted the new recruit out of his office to show him around. "You are starting at level 1, like all new recruits. Trust me; I have several level one missions available. Now, you've been briefed on why you're here obviously…"

"I was. I'm here to pay off the company for the rather pricy experiment as long as it was a success and since I'm alive and standing here next to you, I guess it was." Mallarian observed all around, he and every other person in this place were dressed the same; all black tuxedos. Except for a woman, very attractive, she wore a tight black dress and there was also a kid; had to been no older than ten years old, he had on black jeans and matching t-shirt. "Is that kid supposed to be in here Kyle?"

Kyle swiftly turned and signaled the man to shush his tone. "Don't anger him, he's a ruthless one. I'll introduce you to everyone in a minute, as I was saying, the buildings eight stories high, although you do not have access to most of them, this is level two, the sleeping quarters is level five, the danger, practice quarters is on level three. On this floor, over there is the entertainment room, the cafeteria over there, as you know, we are known as a research company to help new Super's cope with their unusual predicament…"

"So how exactly am I going to be paying off this debt? No one's told me that yet." Mallarian still seemed bewildered to being where he was. "I'm thankful for what they did and the opportunity, but what…"

"You really should have read the contract friend." Kyle took a moment to break the news. "We here at Chronos unofficially work for the government and do, off-the-book, missions. But those missions are worth money, like bounties. We specialize in tracking down ruthless or even new Supers and bring them in, not only for their safety but for Normals' as well."

Kyle led the new recruit into the cafeteria. "I assume you know your abilities now and will be able to perform rank one tasks, but if you feel the need, you can always ask for help; since like you, everyone here is either working off a debt, earning a living, or simply just for fun."

Mallarian seemed to be catching on. "So I can ask for help? Like you?"

Kyle chuckled and shook his head as he explained. "Not I, I'm just the liaison for Chronos. I hand out the missions and handle the day-to-day."

Sitting at a nearby table was the same agent they saw earlier and accompanying her at the table was the ten-year-old kid along with two other men; each eating and engaging in a quiet conversation. Across the room sitting all alone was another man, who wasn't wearing the company uniform; he had on blue jeans, a white shirt, and a long brown trench coat. On his face, covering his eyes were a set of high-tech goggles, resembling night vision.

Kyle approached the first occupied table, where four out of the five people in the cafeteria sat. Kyle began the introductions. "Ok, Mallarian, I like you to meet Sue, that's her brother Bryan," Points to the third guy, "and we just call him Super-bat and last but certainly not least, the Kid."

The three guys grunted and gave out a half-ass wave and went back to their conversation. Sue looked up, gave him a polite smile, and said it was nice to meet him.

Kyle went on to explain that it wasn't like they were disrespecting him. This job was hard; new people came and left all the time. No point in wasting the time getting to know the fresh meat unless they stuck around long enough.

Mallarian then turned his attention towards the lone man and asked. "What about him?"

A bit hesitant, Kyle declined and explained. "I suggest we don't bother him unless you really need to. And even then, I'd have a good excuse. Maverine just likes to be left alone..."

Mallarian instantly recognized the name and stopped Kyle from continuing. "Maverine you say, you don't mean the actual Maverine; world's most wanted and dangerous Super?"

Kyle held his finger over his mouth and whispered. "I wouldn't mention it to him if you talk to him. He's not keen on hearing the old days." He started to head back towards his office. "But come, we'll get you going on your first mission."

Mallarian was hesitant to comply, he just got here and hadn't learned all that he could do. He had a crash course, but it was only an hour. There was a pile of papers in his room on the nightstand he was told to read over, but figured it was all that nonsense paperwork; he was starting to regret not skimming through it at least.

This wasn't his first encounter with Kyle. That was around a few months ago when he first heard the news about his legs. The Doctor told him that he would never walk again. That was until Mister Peterson along with Kyle came into his room and gave him an alternative choice.

They told him that they could give him the serum that granted Normals superpowers. He recalled that it had been banned months prior, but Kyle assured him that they figured out the bugs. Mallarian didn't need to give it much thought and didn't hesitate to say yes. Of course, there were stipulations to go with it, but there was just something about Kyle that made him not care.

They were back inside Kyle's cluttered office where he handed Mallarian a folder. Wasting no time, he opened it up to see just a picture of a man, a location, and a name. Gadget-man with his last known whereabouts. Other than those two things, the folder and paper were empty. Mal's curious eyebrow rose with suspicion as he asked. "Ok, not much in the details huh?"

Kyle wasn't trying to be mean but came across that way. "What can I say, rank one, you are on a need to know basis; and you don't need to know too much. What you need to know is there in front of you. This man stole some sophisticated technology and we want you to retrieve it. There is a supped up van and data on his computer; get them back, eliminate Gadgetman… simple as that."

Shocked, Mal replied quickly. "I thought we were about bringing in Super's and helping them? I don't know if I can eliminate targets…"

"Gadget-man isn't a Super, actually he's a ruthless man who hunts Supers and eliminates them. More importantly, he stole something vital from us and we want it back. The man upstairs tagged this as a high priority. I figured it involved a non-Super, simple task; ease you into things."

Kyle could sense the hesitation coming from the man standing in front of him. He rested his hand on Mallarian's shoulder and said. "Just do the mission. Collect the money, pay off this debt."

Mallarian felt the hesitation subside within him. He nodded, took the document, and got ready for his very first mission with Chronos.

As Mal was heading out the door, Kyle felt the need to add one last thing. "Just remember that we wish these endeavors remain in the shadows from the public. There's a lot of discrepancy with Supers right now and wouldn't want to jeopardize and make matters worse for us as a whole."

SUPERS: GADGETMAN

Mallarian rode his motorbike through the busy streets of Megalopolis and made his way to the outskirts of town. The one side of the road was residential and across the road, the factory district. Gadgetman's hideout was rumored to be located around there and Mal had no real trouble figuring out which one since it stuck out from the rest of the warehouse sector.

There across the street stood a three-story building with no windows on the main floor but had boarded up windows on the upper levels. What set it apart from the rest was the well-kept grass-lawn and a freshly painted white picket fence that surrounding the front perimeter. Down the alley, to the right side of the warehouse, Mal saw a garage door with a smooth paved driveway leading from there back to the street.

Mal kept a keen eye on the building as he thought of a good plausible way of accessing the building; he looked up towards the roof. "I bet this guy suspects someone would be coming for him. And since he goes by the name, Gadget Guy, I'll just assume he's rigged the obvious choices."

Mal had a good arsenal of new abilities, even though, in a world where people like him are known, he didn't like displaying what he could do. With the pressing issues with Supers, most stuck to the shadows or avoid the SBU and City Heroes.

So, he ducked into an alleyway and lifted off into the air. He made a flyover pass to get a good look at the rooftop of the building in question. A fire escape door and vent shaft were the only two ways in from the roof.

Mal used his keen vision to zoom in closer to examine the shaft and saw faint red beams crisscrossing throughout the duct, and he could only assume, they were lasers. So that left one viable option on the roof.

Mal touched down and found the surface rather sticky. He tried to pry his feet free but found some resistance. After struggling with the sticky substance for a few seconds, he felt a sudden surge of electricity strike him. After a minor jolt, he used his superhuman strength to break free and just hover over the sticky surface.

While cursing under his breath, motion sensory mini-guns popped out of each of the four corners, got a target lock on him, and fired a short burst of lead. Luckily Mal had a tough hide and the bullets bounced off but left nasty welts behind. Frustrated, Mal flew straight for the door, fists first, intending to breakthrough.

He rammed it, but the reinforced steel door only slightly caved in. It was enough of a budge to trigger the tripwire on the other side. After a small well-placed explosion erupted, the steel door flew straight into Mal and both landed on the opposing warehouse roof.

"Ok," Mal shoved the door from on top of him, stood tall, dusting himself off. "I'm sick of this gadget guy now." Without another thought, he jerked forward, flying into the freshly blown open door.

He zigzagged around, barely avoiding the sensory guns unleashing hot bullets. Mal kept off the ground as he flew down the stairs to the third floor, down the hall, skipping the three closed doors on either side and straight towards the stairs leading to the second floor all the way to the bottom floor.

He set down at the top of the final staircase, looking to stay quiet and get a read on where this guy might be hiding. As he set down, the stairs instantly turned inward and were now a slide; Mal was caught off guard and slid down, hitting the floor rather abruptly.

Rubbing his neck, Mal scanned the darkened area and just barely catching a glimpse of a man in a heavily armored suit. The mystery individual didn't waste time.

"Are you working for them?"

Confused, Mal asked. "You mean Chronos?"

"I'll take that as a yes." Just as he said that he tossed two smoke bombs towards his victim and drew from his belt, two unique and heavily modified weapons. One was a highly modified shotgun but instead of bullets, shot energy and the weapon fired mini-darts.

Before he could react, Mal had been completely engulfed in smoke and could no longer see the man he was sent here to apprehend. But Gadgetman, using his special helmet, could see fine. He brought up the infrared sensors and knew exactly where the intruder stood. Using the special dart gun, he fired off a dart.

Without the ability to see, the dart had no problem striking its victim. Mal removed the object and quickly realized why this dart gun was so special. Mal found himself now without his gifts, back to his old self before his super being procedure.

Mal was beside himself, not only could he not see his attacker and since he was without his powers, meant he was in deep trouble. Did this serum have a duration he thought, and for how long?

Gadgetman stepped closer, knowing he had this intruder exactly where he wanted him now. "You picked the wrong person to come after chum, but don't take this personally; this is strictly business."

He aimed with the shotgun, taking his time to ensure a direct hit.

But before Gadget man could fire, from behind, out of nowhere, the Kid suddenly appeared, like he was invisible before. With a wicked grin, he held out both hands and a bright bold blue surge of energy shot out and blasted straight through his victim's chest. Gadgetman hit the floor.

Mal, who was bracing for the shot, opened his eyes. And when the gas finally dissipated, he saw the giddy Kid, tea-bagging the deceased.

The Kid boasted with joy. "I totally just owned that guy, you should have seen it, bro!"

Confused but grateful, Mal replied. "Um, thanks for the help."

"No sweat man, I won't tell Kyle you needed my help, not if you cut me in the reward."

"Sure, but why were you following me?"

The Kid replied as he pushed the corpse and rolled it over to inspect his pockets. "I wanted in on getting this guy and I had nothing better to do at the time."

Mal searched the remainder of the floor. It was a large open area, a small room off by the stairs, and a giant heavily armored van across the way. Mal remembered the file, he was to obtain files and a super van; this must be the one it was referring to. He also recalled something about getting back files on a computer; maybe that was in the other room.

Mal knelt and checked Gadgetman's pockets, there inside he found keys; possible van keys. He looked to the Kid and asked. "Do you know anything about computers?"

"Yeah dude, I totally play X-box like ten hours a day."

"Ok, I'll go check out that room there, see if that's where his computer is. Are you old enough to drive?"

The Kid in return just glared because he wasn't impressed. This ten-year-old wasn't like any other, he could blast an energy hole through metal. Before he got angry enough to do something stupid, Mal smiled and tossed over the keys.

As the Kid made his way towards the van, Mal reached the room. Kicking the door open, inside he saw a giant supercomputer. Over by the van, the Kid made his way to the opposite side of the van and located the only door, which was on the side of the van. There was a keyhole so he inserted the key. Just seconds after turning the key to unlock it, the entire van exploded.

Spinning around to asset what went wrong, Mal saw the translucent Kid walk from out of the fiery mess that was once the van. He was walking through it unharmed like he was a ghost.

The Kid wasn't impressed, but his quarrel wasn't with Mal, but the man he already killed. "Not cool man. I really hate this guy." Not long after the van blew up, the computer followed suit.

Mal had a smirk as he shook his head. "Now I hate this guy. I don't think Kyle's going to like this."

SUPERS: GARGOYLE

Mallarian arrived back at the Chronos building alone and empty-handed. Once he got off the elevator and made it back to Kyle's office to deliver his report, out stepped Kyle who seemed rather pleased to see him back.

"Mal, you're alive; great work." Even though it sounded cold and disconcerted, Kyle said with a smile and pizzazz. Kyle then asked. "How did your first mission go?"

"To be perfectly honest, not so well I'm afraid. He rigged the van and computer to explode if tampered with…"

"So you were unable to retrieve the stolen data I take it." Kyle didn't bat an eye or come across angry. He changed the subject like it never happened. He handed Mal another file. "Ok, onward to your second mission then." Kyle walked him back to the elevator and went over the mission quickly. "This one is a Super; time is not on our side. Witnesses have spotted the seemingly frightened but dangerous Super. From little of what we were able to gather, he's made of stone, looks like a gargoyle, and appears to be running on a rampage."

Mal didn't like going into a bad situation with so little info, but something about Kyle clouded his better judgment. "Ok, well I can fly, so catching up to him won't be an issue. When I do track this Super down, then what?" After his first mission and how it ended, Mal wasn't sure anymore what their agenda was.

Trying to answer without really answering the question, Kyle replied with. "Well, we're not here to kill Supers Mister Mallarian, but to bring them in. But if he resists and you think you have no alternative, well let's just say, it's better to have one less dangerous Super out there. Just remember to be discreet about it."

Flying through the air, Mal had a great view of the city. It was a port as well, the ocean surrounding the east and southeast perimeter. To the Northeast was publicly known as SBU Island; the prison where they brought any and all Supers and those deemed as villains remained. But for a small few like Mallarian, who until recently wasn't a Super, he had no clue or reason to know who the SBU was. He mostly kept to himself and his private endeavors.

Mal had the last known whereabouts of this gargoyle Super and was almost there. With his keen sight and flight advantage, he was able to see off in the distance, the mass destruction and disturbance this gargoyle without question caused. The path eventually led him back to the abandoned warehouse district where Gadgetman's hideout was, but this time, at the opposite end. He was able to track the gargoyle to an unfinished building surrounded by construction equipment and vehicles.

Mallarian landed on the incomplete roof, which was about ten floors high, and about to engage when he saw two luxury unmarked sedans pull up to the locked gates of the construction site. Curious he asked himself, "I wonder who they are."

Mal remained up top and out of sight as he watched four men in black suits exited from the back of the sedans and use some sort of gadget to snap the chain with ease. After they opened the gate, both cars pulled in and the men in groups of two wasted no time and stormed the building.

Mal then had to listen as he heard them yelled out to the presumed gargoyle target. "We're with the SBU, come in peacefully." Mal stepped back and tried to think, who were these SBU guys? And why were they here to apprehend the same guy he was here for? It didn't matter, apparently, the gargoyle guy didn't care as he then heard gunfire and the sounds of grunts and groans followed by the sounds of bodies smacking against cement.

Mal didn't quite know what to do. But he knew his mission and was adamant about sticking to it. After all, he certainly didn't want to fail his second mission. He wasn't going to let a few Normals in cheesy suits get in the way of that. So he flew down and landed on the level where the commotion was taking place. As a dazed SBU agent landed next to him, Mal saw the gargoyle engaged in hand to hand range with two agents as the third was readying himself to fire her special service weapon. But since the gargoyles skin was made of stone, the darts just harmlessly bounced off.

The gargoyle knocked out another agent as he flung him across the room. The one agent shooting noticed Mal standing there and aimed with her special weapon. "Freeze, SBU, who are you?"

Stammering to answer, Mal didn't quite know the protocol here for Chronos. Then the word "discreet" entered his mind. He pointed at the stone creature and said. "I'm here for him."

With a nod, she fired a dart that struck Mal once again in the chest. And like before, when he pulled it out he found himself without his new abilities.

The gargoyle saw Mal and knew the fate this guy would face if he didn't help him, even though he knew his intentions. But what he wasn't certain about, was he there to help or capture. But a fellow Super was in danger and he'd figure out afterward. So the gargoyle jumped in front to protect him from further harm. It didn't take long for the stone creature to finish off the agents and leave them unconscious when their backup arrived.

He brought Mal to the roof where they could talk alone. The gargoyle had a gruff tone. "And who are you? I figured out you ain't with them."

Mal felt his abilities slowly coming back, he answered. "No, I have no clue who those guys were. I work for a company named Chronos; we help and protect Supers."

The stone creature eyed Mal up and down, trying to get a read of him; seeing if it was lying or not. He said. "I've never heard of any Chronos. And you seriously don't know who the SBU is? You're a Super right? Every Super should know who they are."

Mal mentioned. "Well, I've only been a Super for a few weeks. Still got lots to learn I guess."

The Gargoyle seemed tired. "So you guys help out Supers huh? To recruit, or hide from them?"

"I think both, still not sure. I'm the new guy. They helped me when all hope was lost." Mal smirked as he said next. "Come on, if you don't like it, you could always leave. You are made of stone and have impressive strength."

The gargoyle knew time wasn't on their side but knew the SBU wouldn't stop their relentless pursuit and still hesitant, he eventually nodded. "Ok, I'll follow you."

The elevator doors of the Chronos building opened and right there to greet Mal and his new friend was Kyle along with two men in lab coats. Mal was the first to step off and Kyle motioned for his stone friend to stay on. "My associates here will escort you to level 4." The gargoyle eyed Kyle up and down and felt that this was the one man you could definitely trust.

The two associates joined the gargoyle on the elevator just as the doors closed, leaving a very curious Mal alone with Kyle. Mal had to ask. "What's on the fourth floor?"

Kyle answered but kept it concise. "It's where we get to know the capabilities of new Supers and get them settled in."

Mal had to address the agents he encountered. "Hey Kyle, there were these men in suits there too. And they had the same crap that the gadget guy had…"

A concerned Kyle cut in. "Those are SBU agents. Didn't you pay attention to your training? You were briefed on how to handle them. Each agent carries a special gun, which shoots darts, inside those darts is serum. Now what that serum does, it temporarily negates a Super of his powers. it doesn't last too long, but long enough to give them an advantage over you. I suggest you don't get hit by them."

While rubbing his chest, Mal replied. "Yeah, I recall reading up on them. I just didn't know they had that kind of firepower. Maybe I should have read the entire document huh."

"Believe me, if it was another day, I'd tell you to take the rest of the day to read up on the stuff you probably didn't listen to during your briefings. But we're short on men and I really need you to continue working. But I have to hand-deliver this folder to the man upstairs pronto. Why you take this time to grab something to eat, I'll be right back."

Mal nodded and replied. "Ok, I'll go ask someone in the cafe to catch me up while I wait."

Mal made his way into the cafeteria, where he found the same people hanging out as before. Like always, the same bunch sat at the one table while the one kept to himself across the room. The Kid wasn't present; perhaps he was out on his own mission.

He went to join the group of three, but the one called Bryan used his foot to pull the chair he was about to sit in away and coldly said. "This chair's taken."

Mal didn't want to start an argument, so he nodded and made his way over to the lone individual. Maverine was minding his own business, reading the paper through those high-tech looking goggles shielding his eyes. Mal didn't know why he always wore them, never really bothered to ask. Maybe it was a good question to help break the ice between them.

As he joined from across the table, Mav didn't even look up to acknowledge his presence. Mal started to talk. "So, you're the Maverine huh; what's with the goggles?"

Maverine wasn't known to be a conversationalist. Without tilted his attention away from his readings, Mav replied. "Look… friend; I'm not looking to get all chummy with the fresh help. If you need a hand on a mission, sure, you can ask me, I'll help no questions asked. But this whole, getting to know you crap, save it for the ones who care." After turning the page in his book he added. "And to clarify that last part, that's no one here in this building."

Mal took the subtle hint as he nodded and replied. "Ok, I see why you sit alone now."

An irritable Mav diverted his attention towards the annoying nuisance at his table. If it wasn't for those goggles, his death glare would be most fearful. "Listen, whatever your name is, I'm not going to get to know every Joe-blow that enlists here. Do you know how many recruits come and go around here? Yeah, I gave up counting too." Mav then extended his hand and continued before Mal had the chance to shake it. "I'm Maverine; call me Mav, the destructive asshole no one wants to fuck with. You need my help, just ask. Now if you aren't going to shut up and eat, go pester someone else."

Mal got up and headed to grab some grub. When he returned with his tray, he found an empty table and sat down. As he was about to bite down into his sandwich, Sue, the only female on the premise spontaneously appeared in the seat across from him. It was known that she was a teleporter, but it still surprised Mal.

Sue was quite beautiful and talked like a person who cared for everyone. "Don't let them bother you. They're just teasing you because you're the new guy." She extended her gesture and Mal graciously accepted it. "I'm Sue; the one who pulled the chair away is my brother Bryan. The other guy is Michael, but we just call him Superbat. The youngest is my son, Billy, but likes to be called the Kid."

Mal was surprised to hear the son part and remarked without realizing he did. "Wow, you must be a proud mom. That kid is insane..." He then apologized for misspeaking.

"No need, I know this isn't the life for him. But as you can tell, no one tells him what to do. He's fueled with hatred; he's egotistical and determined to be known as the most feared Super out there."

Kyle had returned with multiple folders in his hand. He requested to speak with both Sue and Bryan in his office and handed the Bat one of the folders. Mal was now practically alone since the only other person present kept to himself. Confused, he thought Kyle had a mission for him and followed them to his office.

As he peeked through the window, all he saw was Kyle alone in his office, with his head tilted down reading over some files. He knew Sue had the ability to teleport, so assuming she took Bryan with her wasn't farfetched. Mal gave the door several gentle knocks and proceeded inward before getting the official go-ahead. Kyle seemed flustered as he scrambled to closed and conceal the files he was reviewing. "Aw Mister Mallarian, I have a good one just for you." He stood up and came around his desk to greet Mal. "I hope you're good to go."

Mal sensed there was something Kyle was hiding but didn't feel the need to quench his curiosity. After a nod, Kyle smiled and handed the closest file from his desk into Mal's hands. "Have a seat; this one is going to be a little more difficult."

When both parties were seated comfortably, Kyle proceeded to explain the details. "This case takes priority above the rest. If I didn't have the others already out on other missions, I'd take all hands on deck for this." Mal opened the file as Kyle continued on and saw the picture of an older grizzly looking fellow who was called Tom Wolfganger. Not too much surprise, there wasn't a lot of information in this file. Chronos didn't like sharing especially with those who were new and not yet trusted with sensitive information. All the paper had was just his last known whereabouts, which happened to be a logged cabin in the huge dense forest south of the city.

"He's has stolen Chronos property. A pair of wolves we've been extensively doing superhuman testing on; with much success, I may add. But without their daily shot, they will die. So go retrieve the specimens and apprehend, subdue the culprit."

After standing up, Mal remarked. "Best place to start is the cabin I take it?"

SUPERS: WOLFGANGER

The forest was to the South of the city and it was thick and huge; spreading several kilometers wide and about double that in length. There was a lovely crystal blue lake in the middle with a river running along the east side which led into the ocean. Mal knew it would be easier to survey the area by flying overhead and hoped that the cabin would be somewhere near the lake, along the tree line; making it visible from above.

When he was out of the building and away from Kyle, Mal started to think clearly again. What was going on here; something wasn't adding up. What really happened with the gargoyle guy, and why wasn't he more upset about his failed mission? But the more he tried to think, that echo of Kyle's voice grew louder and the less he thought and just wanted to do what was asked.

Many cabins were along the shoreline of the lake, Mal figured that if this guy did kidnap some raged-out wolves, he'd probably want to remain isolated. He saw one that seemed to fit the needs of Wolfganger better and set down a few hundred meters away; figuring sneaking in on foot might be the better choice.

While he silently moved through the thick bush, cautiously avoiding twigs and leaves to ensure his quiet approach, Mal heard the heavy panting of what could only be described as a hungry wolf; multiple ones coming from behind him.

Mal paused as he was unsure of two things; were these the beasts he was here to retrieve and did they knew of his presence. Up ahead, towards the big trees, a grizzled voice answered those suspicions.

"So, I see they sent the fresh meat for me, how thoughtful." Out stepped a stocky, well-built man, with dark greying hair with a matching untrimmed beard. He sniffed the area where Mal stood and after a toothy grin, he continued. "You reek of Chronos. I smelt your scent the moment you flew into the forest. A friendly tip if you somehow live through this; next time approach from upwind."

His mutated wolves began to stalk their prey, each stepping to opposing sides in order to flank Mal. These pair of wolves weren't just enhanced through gene-splice enhancing, they also possessed some cybernetic implants. Half of their skull was replaced; their one eye now robotic, half of their ribcage replaced with a metal exoskeleton as well as their front legs, which had razor-sharp blades replacing their claws. Ferocious and powerful beasts they had now become, something a Super wouldn't want to cross, let alone two of them.

Tom told his wolf companions, "It's chow time boys, enjoy." And with that said, he stepped back behind the tree and disappeared. Mal spun around to face his two wolf stalkers and took a defensive stance, allowing them to make the first move.

"Ok fellows, I'm here to bring you back. No one here needs to get hurt."

The wolves didn't seem to understand or care for what Mal was saying. As the drool frothed from their hungry mouths, the wolves slowly waited to make their attack. The one couldn't wait and lunged forward. With its powerful hind legs, it made a gigantic and swift leap for its intended victim. But Mal was on the ready and had no trouble sidestepping the attack.

Now, with both beasts on totally opposite sides, Mal had to keep moving his head back and forth, ensuring he could react if either one made a move. And they did, simultaneously lunging for their prey. Mal did the only thing he could and bolted straight up into the air. His feet just barely dodged the vicious claws as both of his attacker's collided headfirst into one another.

Mal stuck to hovering in the air, figuring they could leap that high as he came up with a new plan to capture and bring these things in alive. He didn't want another failed mission on his record, failed missions didn't pay off the debt. Not to mention, what might happen to him if he kept failing. He was one for two and wanted to increase his success rate.

Mal stayed above to figure out a better plan as the two dazed and injured wolves took a moment to regain focus. From out of nowhere in the treetops, Tom pounced towards his prey, catching him off guard. Tom "The Wolf" Wolfganger had some pretty deadly claws of his own and gouged them straight into the side of the flying man.

Both men hit the ground hard as Mal forcefully shoved Tom off and into a nearby tree. Checking his gushing wound, Mal knew over time, it would heal, and staggered to his feet. Just as he got to his feet, Tom did as well and with self-assurance, boasted. "You shouldn't come to a claw party unarmed my friend."

Mal, knowing he needed to act, replied. "Who says I'm unarmed?" And without hesitation, Mal reached towards the open air next to him and ripped through. A flash of a faint red light illuminated and when it was gone, Mal had in his hands two matching .45 caliber pistols. He took aim but didn't fire. "Now, just let me take back what you stole and come in peacefully."

"I rather die than let Chronos get their mitts back on…" Tom then suddenly charged with his claws out, ready to rip Mal apart. But Mal retaliated by unleashing several bullets in each pistol, all of them striking the target's chest. As Tom dropped to the ground and Mal spun right around to take aim at the furious wolves.

The animals didn't want to back down. They weren't intimidated by the weapons directly aimed at them and just charged forth. Against his better judgment, but didn't want to end up dinner, Mal emptied each of the clips. Some of the random bullets harmlessly bounced off as they struck the metal hide, but those that didn't, penetrated the skin and hit the heart. As the smoke left the hot barrels, Mal found himself standing over three dead bodies.

With a long, drawn-out disproving sigh, he muttered, "Just great, another failed mission."

He dragged the body of Tom over to the logged cabin and quickly dug a grave; hoping to hide the evidence and to make sure no one could find him. When he turned back to dump the body, Tom was gone. Confused and now on edge, Mal spun completely around expecting an attack.

Mal stuck out his hand and reached into his pocket dimension, pulling out his Japanese Katana. With both hands firmly gripped to the handle, he kept it close and on the ready. "I knew he seemed too easy to take down."

Mal hovered a few feet off the ground, to quietly float around, hoping he could spot some tracks that might lead him to the person in question. As he found an obvious footprint, he took a second to examine it.

Bursting out from the cabin door, a hulking Tom dove straight for him. But Tom's appearance was different; he was more wolf-like than before. Complete with fangs, a snout, and an extra hundred pounds of solid muscle, he tackled Mal out of the air.

After dealing with another nasty gash across his victim's chest, Mal was able to parry the next onslaught of vicious slashes with the sword. But Tom's superior strength and quickness were too much to match. With a ferocious slash from his claws, Tom disarmed Mal who then was able to reverse somersault back to avoid a duel-clawed attack.

"You should have rejected the mission." Tom snarled, stepping to the side as he stalked his prey.

Mal stayed on the defensive, preparing for an attack when he replied. "If you didn't steal Chronos property, I wouldn't be here."

With a toothy grin, Tom replied. "Is that what they told you?" And before Mal could ask more, Tom lunged with both claws ready to tear him apart. But Mal took to the air and barely avoided the claws once more. With his palms held out, a greenish discharge of energy emerged and created a fair size hole in the victim's chest.

Once again, the Wolf hit the ground but this time, Mal picked up his blade and used it to remove the head, ensuring he wouldn't get up the second time. He finished burying the evidence and carry both mutated wolf corpses back to Chronos HQ.

The elevator ride up, Mal thought over what the Wolf said to him. Was he lying to lower his guard or was he telling the truth? As the doors slid open, there to greet him upon another completed mission was Kyle. He even seemed pleased that Mal was able to bring back the specimens, even if they were deceased. Kyle motioned to keep both wolves on the elevator and when the doors closed behind, Kyle started to brief him on another important endeavor.

"Congratulations, truly remarkable work Mallarian. But there's no time for a debriefing." Kyle seemed uneasy with what he was about to say next. "The others are out on a case and are in dire need of some backup. I would send in Maverine, but he's off on his own case. I need all hands on deck here Mal."

Concerned for the safety of the others, Mallarian pressed on. "You were right; it's a hectic day for sure. What's wrong, where do I need to be?"

"Sources told us that our sister company, the Beginning, has turned on us. Our inside man had stumbled upon a plan to invade our building and slaughter us tonight while we sleep. Their greed for power has taken control; they want the research we possess solely for their own selfish agenda. We cannot allow that, so the others went ahead without you."

Something didn't sit well with what Kyle was saying. Mal tried to remember, before joining Chronos, when he was normal. He recalled reading up on when Supers first started to surface with the public, one of them, a female Super, Ami, something, announced that she was going to start a foundation that would welcome in scared and confused new Supers and help them cope. But that memory vanished and he felt obligated to do what Kyle asked.

Kyle once again said. "Get over there and give our people any necessary aid. It's a war out there so don't feel hesitant to hide your abilities."

When Mal received the coordinates of the building in question, he left. Flying straight through the air, Mal saw the building where he was to meet up with the others. It was on fire and on the verge of collapsing. As he flew closer, an explosion on one of the upper floors erupted. Smashing through the window, the bloody body of Superbat shot out and sailed across the road and landed hard on the opposing building's rooftop.

Mal joined up with the Bat, and as he landed, Sue appeared. Mal was seeking answers. Superbat, who was barely conscious, offered some. He didn't speak much, but when he did, in this form, it was raspy and deep. "The Kid's still inside with Bryan. We were able to neutralize most, but some of them are pretty damn tough."

Down below, a large crowd of Normals had already gathered. Some were taping the events and uploading them to the Net. Off in the distance, the sounds of sirens blared, it was only a matter of minutes before the SBU made an appearance. And none of them wanted to be on the scene when they did.

With the Bat critically injured, Sue took him and ported out. Mal was now alone while the fighting continued in the building across the way. Since he wasn't sure what to expect, he pulled out his pistols and flew across to the building's roof.

Upon landing, there to greet him was a beautiful slender built Japanese woman, wielding a finely crafted edged weapon. Engraved on the weapon, were Japanese runes of sorts. Mal didn't hesitate; he treated this person like a hostile and opened fire. With a swift movement, the young woman sidestepped and parried the incoming bullets with ease.

Mal was still injured from the previous encounter with the Wolf and couldn't react as fast as a healthy version of himself. But he was needed and injured or not, he was still willing to help. He continued to fire the spray of bullets, adjusting the aim as he watched this young lady weaved in and out of the line of bullets and if one looked like it was going to strike, the blade of the sword swatted it away.

Each bullet fired, Mal took a step back, trying to keep a two-blades distance between him and his opponent. But the roof was only so long and his opponent sure was fast. The enraged girl finally caught up to Mal and with one fluid motion, used the blade to slice the pistols in half. As she was about to thrust the blade into Mal's chest, he took to the air, barely avoiding the attack.

Mal shot some of that energy from his hands to keep her occupied as he drew out his sword. He saw the runes once more and thought, maybe the sword is special, and that's where she's drawing her power from. He landed, parried the first attack, and responded with a subtle sweep-kick, and brought his blade up, striking her hands. Her sword flung up out of her grasp and as it sailed back down. The girl let loose a crafty grin as she thought she'd catch the blade as it came back down. But Mal opened his portal to allow the weapon to drop in and immediately shut it.

The poor girl dropped to a knee, her power fizzled from within. Mallarian took the moment and started the interrogation. "What the heck is going on here? Why are you plotting to attack us?"

Surprised by his accusations, the girl chuckled. "Are you naïve or something? You're the one attacking us!"

"Because our spies say you're working against us…"

She continued to chuckle, she found it hard to breathe and get out the words. "You're way over your head aren't you? You seriously have no clue who you're working for."

With his blade pointed directly at her, he replied. "Enlighten me then."

She took a moment to collect herself. After several deep breaths, she was ready to explain the truth. Just as she opened her mouth to start, a blast from a familiar bold blue energy blasted through her chest, leaving quite the hole.

As the fresh body fell, Mal didn't need to but double-checked to see who the culprit was. Standing there with a most wicked grin was the Kid. Mallarian couldn't help but raise suspicion; *did he shoot her on purpose so I wouldn't learn the truth, or did he think he was saving his neck?*

"Again I saved your neck. These people are dangerous; don't let your guard down man." The Kid approached an uneasy man. Mal didn't see the need to kill them, especially not before you got some answers as to why.

"I had the situation contained; I was just seeing what she knew."

"What she knew, who cares. They want us dead but we got them first."

Mal was enraged, he was looking for the truth and it seemed these Chronos people wanted to keep him in the dark.

The Kid could see the anger quickly building up and reacted accordingly. "Just chill dude, it's the job. The rest are dead and Bryan said the SBU baddies are here, so we better jet." The Kid turned back into his translucent self; in this ghost form, he was hard to see and was able to float through solid objects. "Meet up with you back at the HQ dude." He dropped down and vanished.

Mal dropped down out of sight in the alleyway and left the scene, after all, he didn't want to be caught by the SBU and have to explain all of this. Since truthfully, he didn't know anything.

SUPERS: PONGO

This is case file number one-forty-seven: My file. Yeah, I should be the one who is dead, but luckily I was not at home when Peterson sent in his goons to finish me off. I can only assume I got too close to Chronos. Trust me he'll pay, one way or another. I will find the evidence I need to bring him and his organization down. I know I don't have special powers, which is why I'm writing this letter to you... Funny, I never thought I would since in our past, we've had plenty of disagreements. But I trusted the wrong person and now no longer with the SBU... Let me break down what you missed since your days in the SBU:

As you know, like my father, I too joined the Super Being Unit. It's gone through a big change since the new Director arrived only a few years ago. We still investigate all bizarre/Super sounding cases but instead of working alongside you Supers, we police them. We have used gene-augmentation and super technology to aid us. So normal people protecting one another, the way it should be. We both know how loyal and dependable a Super can be.

Fallen agents and those who have been critically injured who have signed up for special projects are experimented on. Through chemicals, they are enhanced and we use cybernetics to replace the missing limbs and organs. But that's nothing compared to what Peterson's scientists have uncovered.

We are equipped with a special dart gun that injects a Super with this serum that temporarily negates their abilities. It may only last a few minutes, but it's enough to give us a slight edge.

You Supers proved time and time again to be unreliable and power-driven so in the end, you couldn't be trusted.

As we both know what happened in the fallout between you and my father, I don't want to get into that right now, we have more pressing matters. While in the SBU, we wanted to stop future Supers from being made, so I had the infamous cat burglar known as the Chameleon hack into the Chronos mainframe and steal the supposedly "improved" super being project files.

But that plan went South and when I met up with him months down the road, he informed us of the truth behind Peterson's company Chronos. When I dug into it more, that's when he had my family slaughtered.

I fear my suspicions are right and Peterson is constructing a most devious plan. He is collecting every and all Supers, not to help, but to stick into a comatose state where they insert needles and draw out their DNA for their scientists to examine and more importantly, experiment.

Chameleon is living proof that he finally was able to grant Normals superpowers. There have been rumors of two others, but nothing is confirmed on my end.

The SBU started an investigation, but after Venkman rallied the government to start up a Super Hero Group, we got sidelined. And we both know the juvenile detectives they are and overwhelmed with the criminal Supers to handle something and I quote your brother, "Not a valuable threat at the moment." So, I'm pleading with you that this one time, you listen and help us out before he completes his most diabolical plan.

So after being fired for being the one who started the unofficial investigation, I decided to do my own digging. This is the last day I'm going to let Peterson roam free. I'm going to do everything in my power to make sure he pays for everything he has done. But I need help.

● ● ●

The two Supers I had to infiltrate Chronos, I haven't heard back from. I have to assume, they've been compromised. That is what you get when you send in a Super to do a Normal's job. But how is Peterson strong-arming them? Or are they betraying me like every other Super I've come across?

I was able to reach William W. Wells Jr., one of a trio of geniuses who is responsible for creating the weapons, gadgets, and vehicles the SBU uses to help combatant the Supers. His twin brother is working with Peterson, helping him create the super being data. We don't know why, but he is.

But we found our in. I had William mask as his brother, forge his credentials and walk into Chronos. From there he was able to steal the data and upload a virus that wiped their computers clean so they couldn't continue on with the project.

His alias, Gadgetman, is a well-respected bounty hunter who works for the SBU from time to time. He's been responsible for apprehending many Supers and mostly the level 4 or higher ones too. So he's been hiding out in his fortified bunker waiting for my arrival.

So that's where I start my day. The first step I need to fight back against Chronos. It'll be much easier to stop Peterson as long as he doesn't have an army of Supers at his disposal. Plus, we have too many egotistical Super beings at the moment, we don't need anymore. Maybe if they were goodhearted and wanted to do good, I'd consider it.

But I woke up feeling good; I just know this is going to be the day everyone will remember.

In my beaten down sedan, I finally was able to get to the warehouse district where William said to meet. He and his family have a building down here, where they do their work. He forewarned me to not approach the front, the roof, the garage, which pretty much do not approach the building itself. Instead, he gave me directions to a safe route only he and his siblings knew. But as I pulled up to the building, I found it half-destroyed; like an explosion happened. Fire-fighters, police, and SBU agents were already on the scene.

What happened here, was he still alive, or did Chronos find out about what he did and send their goons to retrieve it? I fear the worst has happened and losing all hope that Peterson can be stopped. But he was a well-known expert Super hunter, how'd they get to him? Did he put up a fight and take some with him at least?

I casually made my way over to get a better look, hopefully, figure out what exactly went down. I still have a few friends within the SBU so I figured I get some kind of reason as to what might have happened.

I waved my old buddy Bill over and when he could, he snuck past the police tape. "Hey Bill, thanks for seeing me. What happened here?"

"Witnesses claimed that a Super with the ability to fly landed on the roof; then heard some gunfire, then an explosion. And after several minutes of hearing nothing, a bigger explosion erupted which brought half the building down."

I was hesitant to ask but knew I had to. "What about any survivors?" My phone began to vibrate in my pocket, but I didn't answer, I just let it go to voicemail. I was trying to get some answers here.

Bill shook his head as he read from his little black notepad. "Sorry, just one deceased. Do you remember Gadgetman? They found him lying on the ground in his high-tech power armor with a huge hole in his chest. From what the lab geeks figure, this Super can expel some powerful energy. Gadgetman had his SBU issued gun in his hand." He continued to read from his book and then asked something I didn't want to answer. "So why are you here? Were you meeting with him? I thought you were forced out of the SBU. You're not still working on that Chronos case, are you? "

I didn't want to drag good agents down with me, so I did my best to keep him out of the loop. But I knew Bill could sense deceit, so I kept it vague. "Yes, he was helping me gather some crucial Intel I need to bring Peterson down for good." I had to give a little if I was expecting anything in return from Bill. I needed to know what happened in there, more importantly, the computer inside.

We, and by we I mean the SBU, have been wanting to get their hands on this superhuman data for months. Ever since we caught the Chameleon after his recent change. The first confirmed successful normal beings who survived and received abilities from Chronos. We studied and questioned him repeatedly until Venkman showed up and recruited him to his hero group. Venkman is always sticking his nose where it doesn't belong. But that's another story for later.

Bill just shook his head, you knew he's heard this story far too many times before. "When are you going to learn Eric, you can't fight him. He's got too much influence with the government and they like that he can get those impossible missions without bureaucracy done. And I'm sorry about your family, but..."

He was right, but I wasn't going to give up, not that easy. I had sacrificed a lot to get this close and I wasn't going to give up and let William down too. But I knew there was nothing more I could gather here; not right now anyway. "I'll give up when the man responsible for not only my family's death but all those innocent victims he used to experiment on, sees justice." Bill was one of those, by the book kind of guys. The real sheep, the, don't ask just do your job, kind. Yeah, I know, really annoying when you're not one of them.

He was then beckoned over by his partner, I wasn't sure of his name as I only met him once before. But with his attention diverted, I was able to snag a peek at his book when he turned to see what his partner wanted. The computer with the data William had and the truck he acquired from Chronos had both sadly been destroyed beyond reconstruction... just like good old Gadgetman, leave no trace evidence if you get compromised. A good tactic unless you're the one seeking said evidence.

I disappeared back to my sedan before Bill turned around to continue his questioning. I had more important things to do, besides, the SBU can solve what happened there and they'll do what they've done in the past, just sweep it under the rug like it didn't. It's why I went solo, too much red tape; like you're constantly walking on eggshells.

But it sounded like Chronos sent their best to retrieve what Gadgetman stole and he was no match to who showed up. But who was it that got the upper hand? Energy blasts and flying abilities, it didn't sound like the ones I know of. A new player in their ranks perhaps? But with the blown-up computer and van in the mix, maybe, just maybe they were not successful in that task. And if that were the case, then Chronos will still be without creating more Supers. This might be a good thing still.

One thing was certain; today wasn't going to be a walk in the park. I needed help. But who could I trust now, the City's Hero group? It's hard to trust a group of arrogant glory-seeking vigilantes that Venkman picked out. Hardly a group I say, and besides, they had their hands full with all the chaos in this city. Supers these days, most just choose the greedy selfish villainous path. Where are the heroes in the mix? Have the public and SBU ridiculed all the good-hearted Supers and forced them into hiding? A real hero wouldn't buckle under the pressure and suck it up and do what is right. I wished some Supers, like Maverine, would get on that track of thinking.

As I pulled away, I remembered I had a miss call and the caller left me a message.

A gritty raspy voice on the other end, one I did not recognize at first. "Is this Pongo, Agent Eric Pongo?" He knew who I was and sounded rather desperate as well. "I'm in a real jam here, I need your help. I worked alongside your father…" There was something I hadn't thought about in years, my father. He wasn't much of one, but that's because he and two Supers back in the day worked together in junction with the government to bring in Supers. One was Maverine, which meant this had to be the infamous Wolfganger.

Before my father passed, he used to tell me bedtime stories which were usually about their adventures. He told me all about Maverine and Wolfganger, what they were capable of; since Supers weren't public news back in those days, I just assumed he was spicing up the story for my amusement. Today I know different.

"I can't get into it over this line in case they're listening in. But I heard you're looking into Chronos, well I got something you might be interested in."

I thought "the Wolf" was on the same side as his pal Maverine; the neutral side. They were the side that didn't want to be bothered with; the side that said "We've done our fair share and now just want to be left alone." And since their reputation dictates them as extremely dangerous and powerful Supers, nobody argued.

So why did Tom call me and why was he interfering with Chronos? I wasn't going to look a gift horse in the mouth. "Remember that logged cabin your father built for you guys when you were young? I'll be there."

Tom then hung up the phone. That wasn't good; I wonder what he was going to say. I didn't want to call back in case he hung up for a reason.

I continued my drive, keeping a keen eye on the mirrors, ensuring that I wasn't being followed. I kept thinking, why would Tom contact me out of all people, what did he want, and was he with Maverine?

I brought my car back to the safe house and made my way across town to the forest. From the edge of the city, I hiked it from there. I was trying to remember exactly where the cabin was, I knew it was on the west side of the lake, about a hundred meters in from the tree line. A long hike through the thick bush, but it was to remain under the radar. The Wolf worked better in the woods, he had special skills. It took me a bit to navigate and find the right cabin. I didn't want to believe it was the one with fresh claw marks and dry blood on the ground just outside, but it was. The door had been kicked open. That meant only one thing, uninvited guests.

With my trusty SBU pistol in hand, I cautiously entered. I had feared the worst, the cabin was empty. No sign of Tom or whoever came and got him. I investigated the outside and perimeter, I found no tracks which could only mean one thing; whoever Chronos sent, can fly and not only that, he must not be working alone, or if he is, he's quite powerful if he was able to subdue the Wolf on his own. Perhaps it was the same person that eliminated Gadgetman.

Another dead-end isn't what I needed right now. Last I heard Maverine was working for Chronos, I just assumed Tom went with him. Was it Maverine who was sent to capture or would he though; kill him?

Just then I got another call and the first thing I did was check the ID. It was from one of the members from the Beginning, Miss Marik's group of extraordinary people. Curious I answered, "Hello?"

The person on the other end was out of breath and seemed on edge when he replied. "Pongo, we're under attack over here. I think it's the goons from Chronos." It was Brad, a bodybuilder turned fighter. He wasn't a Super, like the others, he was just a very skilled Normal. Each of them wanted to join the Beginning to help people, Super and Normal alike. For a while, they worked with the SBU until it was proven that Miss Marik herself possessed super abilities. A liar that one was, if you knew what she could do, you knew exactly why she wanted to "help" her fellow Super.

"Calm down Brad, who's there exactly?" I was too far to come to the rescue, but wanted to know who it was they sent. I was seeking answers and maybe I could help Brad and his crew stop the onslaught. I did have vast knowledge on how to stop certain abilities.

"I don't know, all of them?" I prayed it wasn't all of them, because if it was, there was no helping them. If it was just one or two, depending on who, sure, wouldn't be a problem; unless that included Maverine.

"I see blue energy zipping past me. I know Bryan, the speedy guy is here. That giant bat thing too, I saw him flying overhead."

Of course, it had to be Bryan, the Kid, and Superbat; three of Chronos' deadliest mercenaries on their roster. Just under Mav, their Chronos' go-to guys for special missions. Sure, they might have a slight advantage in numbers, but those three, they were still no match. I didn't have the heart to tell him that though. "Just group up and take them out together, don't be a lone hero. I'm on my way."

I holstered my gun and took a deep breath. I couldn't believe I was about to do it. I swore to never use my father's ring, but I had no choice. From my pocket, I pulled out a beautifully embroidered leather pouch, in it, a hideous silver ring with a yellowish gem attached to it. What did this ring do? It gave me extraordinary powers but at a price. That price is costly because it will slowly drain your life away. It was how my father died. He was only in his mid-forties when the ring sucked him dry. In the short story I got when I was just a teen, the power got to him. I didn't buy it though, my dad was a strong-willed man. He wouldn't abandon mom and I like that. My gut always told me something didn't add up. But I would have to wait to find the answers.

With this ring, I could create powerful constructs using just my imagination. You were only limited by yourself. I'm able to create impenetrable armor and force fields to protect others. I can also fly, shoot bolts of yellow force, and even form gigantic limbs with the strength that compares to some of the strongest of Supers out there. But like I said, all for the price I didn't want to pay as my father did; my life.

I took a deep breath and slipped on the ring. I could instantly feel the power of the ring flowing through my body and it felt good. This wasn't the first time I felt this power, when I was ten, I found my father's ring while he was passed out on the sofa from a long night being out. I was captivated by its aura; I could hear it calling to me. So I tried it on. Since I had no idea what it could do, I accidentally fired off a bolt, destroying the TV and startling my father awake.

Boy was he pissed. Especially when he tried to grab my arm to stop me, I jumped back, the ring erected a field, and a huge fist appeared from nowhere and punched him in the gut. Scared and stunned, I pulled the ring off, gave it back and that's when I made the vow to never wear it again.

Ok, I put it on a few years ago when I was still an SBU agent and practiced, thinking maybe I could harness the power and use it for my job. But I decided against it at the time.

But now I didn't really have a choice; these people were going to die if I didn't. Plus I needed answers to who killed Gadgetman and the Wolf. So I activated the armor and took to the air. The building was all the way across town. But since I was flying, it wasn't going to take me long.

In mid-flight, I was about to collide with a Super who was floating in my path. Suspended in the air, high above the closest rooftop, this poorly homemade costumed individual was striking a commanding pose. I didn't recognize him as a member of the City's Super Squad but figured I better stop, just in case.

"Halt Super, who are you, and what is your business?" Seriously, who was this guy? And who asks those ridiculously cheesy lines?

"I'm Eric Pongo..." I didn't get a chance to continue.

I could tell that this person was only a teenager now, you could hear it in his voice and lingo. "Surrender now or face the dynamic duo, Lock and Load!"

Ok, this was a silly prank or something. I had an important situation to get to. I didn't reply and just continued to fly past this crazy nuisance. He fired a green energy bolt at me and since I didn't expect it, it hit my armor.

"Listen here," I figured trying to reason with him was better than fighting. "I have to be somewhere that needs me; can we postpone this silly endeavor later?"

"You're under arrest for..." He then paused and tapped on his ear. I could only assume, he had a headset on and was talking to his partner, Lock, or Load, whoever the other was. Since he was slightly distracted, I bolted off. I descended down and lost him in the alleyways. That dumb kid just cost me valuable time, the time I didn't have.

I finally got within view of the six-story building which was now on fire, and like Gadgetman's warehouse, half-destroyed. I took a moment to assess everything that was going on because there was so much happening at once. The Normals down below scrambled in fear, the news copters were hovering overhead, taping the entire thing. I even saw SBU snipers on adjacent rooftops, I presume to await orders to fire.

I spotted Superbat on the rooftop; he had just viciously slaughtered one of the Beginning members. I couldn't tell which one from here. He was the only one from Chronos I could see. But considering one was fast, one could be a ghost and one could teleport, he stuck out from the bunch.

Not knowing fully what was happening, I set down on a nearby rooftop and observed. It was no use trying to save the day now, it was looking grim. I did get a glimpse of Sue, the speedster's sister, she would appear behind each of the snipers and subdued them. I guess the rumors of her being a Chronos member were in fact true. It made sense; her brother and son were members, why wouldn't she join? But I remember her being one of those ultra-rare good-hearted Supers and would never want to willingly harm anyone. Had she been converted? It wouldn't surprise me these days, seemed everyone I knew was doing that.

I had to think, was Maverine present or not? Because if he was, then seeking his help wasn't an option anymore, he was corrupted like the rest. It was hard to believe he joined Chronos, but I figured he only did it so he could hide from the SBU since he was number one on the most wanted list.

When the smoke cleared, the fire-fighters finally put the fires out, the Chronos agents were gone and the Beginning personnel was all deceased. I floated down to the ground, removed the ring, and found my old buddy Bill who was now on this scene.

I was right about one thing; this day was going to be remembered...

I didn't get long to find out what happened from Bill. After all, he was busy with the impending chaos I knew for certain would rain down on the Metropolis at any moment. What I didn't tell him was that I was a part of the reason for it. This was the last straw, these people didn't deserve to be slaughtered like this; Peterson is going to pay.

I found out what I wanted to know, Maverine wasn't anywhere near the area. The SBU snipers were specifically looking for him, hoping he out of all the known Supers, would make an appearance. It was time to get back to my safe house and find out something that will help me find the location of Peterson. Or maybe I finally got a response from that letter I sent out earlier in the morning... I can only pray he'll respond.

I have no choice but to involve them now, this is getting out of hand. But before I did, I'm going to need to clear my head, think about nothing except for this mission...

SUPERS: THE HACKER

Mallarian had no issues making his way back to Chronos. Just as the elevator door opened, you could hear someone yelling profusely and it was coming from Kyle's office. Curious, Mal scrambled over to see who it was that was yelling. Through the glass, the big man Maverine was completely irate about something; Mal couldn't quite make it out.

Kyle stood there completely frightened as he tried his best to calm the angered Super down. After a minute, Maverine ripped the door from its hinges and stormed towards the emergency stairs. Mallarian stood to the side in silence, avoiding further conflict with the man. After a minute to let Kyle's nerves calm down, Mal entered.

"Awe, Mister Mallarian, great work out there. Bryan has already debriefed me on the situation at the other building."

Mallarian was furious, and wanted to give the man a piece of his mind but had restrained those feelings. Now he was curious and didn't want to start a confrontation here, not now. He had many questions, but knew Kyle wasn't going to indulge; after all, he's been hiding something all day. Why was Maverine angry, what was the deal with Gadgetman? What happened to that gargoyle thing and two wolf specimens? And most important, what was that girl at the other building talking about?

Kyle continued on like everything was normal and grabbed a folder from his desk. "So, this is good news, you've been cleared for level two missions. The first one to do it within a day; which today is good because we have plenty of riskier jobs that need attending."

"Level two means higher-paying jobs too right; which means I can pay my debt off even faster?"

With a nod to agree with that statement, Kyle added. "Mallarian my friend, the way things are going, as crazy as today is, you might be able to pay that debt off today." Kyle then noticed the bloodstain on Mal's shirt and sought to it. "Are you injured, because as a level two, you now have access to our resident healer and basement?"

Mallarian was flabbergasted, these guys have a healer too; no wonder they can do mission after mission and be unscathed. He was curious about the other thing mentioned too. "The basement, what's down there?"

"That's the weapon shop. Tinkering away down there is the brilliant scientist inventor William Wells. He creates gizmos and weapons to help aid us in our missions. Most just call him Q, you know, because of that infamous British Spy movie a while back."

"I may use the healer before my next mission; which is?" He waited to hear what Kyle had in store for him.

And continued on he did. Kyle handed over the file and began to explain while Mal started to flip through. "On the Web, he's known as the Hacker, but spelled in that fancy Leet format kids do these days. I'll never understand it myself, but, he's hacked into the Chronos system..."

"Let me guess, he's stolen vital information and we don't want that."

"Part of it yes, but our techies did some digging. It appears that Gadgetman wasn't the only one who managed to get their hands on the super-being data before someone wiped it from our system. And since we were unable to recover said data from our first target, we have a second chance. But the techs found something; someone in this city has been making online purchases. Those items combined are similar to the equipment needed to recreate their own lab and create their own Supers."

Mal caught on, surprising more information than previous missions for sure. "And if that is so, they're a great threat, not only us but depending on their motives, everyone." Mallarian wasn't sure what was true or false, but this company, Kyle, did give him a second chance at life, and he did promise to repay them. These thoughts are what kept him going; and the thought of freedom, what would he do first once his debt was paid. "Ok, let me get patched up and I'll set out immediately after."

"Understood, Medik is located on level 3 with the danger room. Her office is to the right once you step off the elevator."

Mal nodded and boarded the elevator. Once it stopped and the doors opened, for the first time Mal found himself on level three, the danger quarters. Here the Supers entered a high-tech room that simulated fights for them to practice their abilities and keep their fighting skills keen. But in case of any injury, the medical ward was just next door.

A strikingly attractive woman with lengthy platinum hair and olive oil skin was just finishing up with another patient. He left in a hurry, bumping Mal in the shoulder as he did. Thinking nothing of it, Mal gently knocked and introduced himself. "Hello, are you Medik?"

She wasn't much for words; after all, she had a job to do. She grabbed Mal by the arm and motioned for him to sit. Without exchanging any words, she placed her hands over his wounds, closed her bright blue eyes, and out radiated a holy white glow from the palms. And seconds later, all his wounds were gone. She immediately sat down and dismissed him.

Concerned for her, Mal asked. "Are you ok, do you need help?"

Her reaction was all he needed, her smile read, "Yeah, as you care." She looked up and saw the sincere concern in his eyes and spoke. Her tone was soft and innocent. "Oh, you're being serious."

"Yeah, I am."

She explained how her abilities worked. "When I heal people, it temporarily drains my life-force. If I heal too many in a row, it puts a toll on me."

"Oh, I'm sorry, I didn't know."

She shrugged it off, playing the tough girl. Secretly she knew Chronos, i.e. Peterson, was listening. "No sweat tough guy, it's my role in all this."

Mal caught on, "Oh, you're paying back your debt too huh?"

Being deceiving, she sarcastically remarked, "Yeah, sure, my debt. Now if you'll excuse me, tough guy, I have to get back to work."

Mal could take a hint that he wasn't wanted when a woman told him, and didn't want any trouble. He graciously thanked her once again and headed back for the elevator and made his way down to see what this "Q branch" had to offer.

Many sub levels under the Chronos building, the elevator finally stopped. When the doors opened it led to a rather large underground facility filled with dozens of assistants and loaded with random highly sophisticated weapons, gizmos, and vehicles.

About ten feet out stood an elderly man in a lab coat. He was balding, wearing some kind of goggle gizmo on his forehead, and resting on his shoulder was an oversized cannon. An assistant was nervously standing next to him, who didn't look confident with what was about to happen.

"Now, you sure you triple checked the wires this time Frankie?"

The assistant sighed when he replied. "Doctor Wells sir, I'm Stuart, not Frankie."

"It's all the same Francis," Wells heard the beep from the elevator and spun around to see who was coming down for a visit. As he spun, the barrel from the cannon spun too, striking poor Stuart in the back of the head, knocking him right out. "Not another one, clean up the aisle... whatever this one was labeled." He tossed the cannon and a hesitant assistant was right there to dive and barely catch the weapon.

With giddy open arms, Wells greeted Mallarian. "Well, if it isn't..." He removed the goggles for a moment to eye the new man up and down. Confused, he asked. "Who are you?"

He extended his hand and introduced himself, "Hello, I'm Mallarian and you must be Doctor Wells."

Mumbling under his breath, Wells staggered away. "Mallaro, Mal... Maverine." He glanced back to assure himself, "You're not Mav, you're not big enough. Plus I think I would know my best customer. He sure likes anything that makes a big boom. And his goggles that protect his eyes; I came up with that. That's right, and they say I'm getting too old for this." He entered his office to gather a few items. "I have his special equipment all ready to go here. But I would like it if he was the one to pick them up." He turned back and added. "Not that I don't trust you, but I don't even know your name."

"Doctor Wells, I'm..."

Taken back a step, the confused Doctor replied. "Wells, that's my name too. And you're a doctor huh, what's your specialty?"

"No, I'm not Wells; I'm Mal-lar-ian!" Mal tried to contain his laughter, he was also frustrated.

"Listen, sonny, I'm not going to be able to pronounce that. Just tell Mav I have his gear and for him to come down himself, don't send his help. I have important work to do down here."

"You've been down here way too long." Mal gave up and headed back for the elevator.

Mallarian flew into the residential section of town and landed a few houses down from the posted address on the document. From a distance, Mal could survey the home belonging to one Ned Carver, aka, the Hacker.

The house was your typical two-story home straight from 1950; a white picket fence, a giant tree complete with a tire swing, freshly cut greener than green grass, and an expensive brand new car in the driveway.

Mal read the file again, Ned was a sixteen-year-old nerd genius; being hated in school, turned to computers when he was younger. Mal thought over a plan. "You know what, he's sixteen, I should just confront his parents and get them to make him turn it over."

Mallarian tossed on his sunglasses, completing the cliché government official look, and casually walked up to the front door and gave it a gentle knock.

The door opened and there to greet him was your typical 50's mom, all cheery and polite. "Good afternoon, how are you today?"

After flashing his fake badge, he replied. "Hello Ma'am, I'm with the government. I'm here to speak with your son, Ned. Is he here?"

"Please, why don't you come in," she opened the door all the way and continued. "I just made a batch of fresh chocolate chip cookies. Mm, don't they smell scrumptious?"

There was something off about this woman; Mal couldn't quite put his finger on it. But she did invite him inside, so he walked in.

There to the left, just inside the living room stood a man in a housecoat, with an old fashion smoking pipe in his hand. "Greetings agent, isn't it a terrific day today?"

Bursting into the room was a young boy, about ten years old. In his hand was a toy car, and he was making vroom noises as he ran into the living area. The mother and father in unison chuckled with the dad remarking. "Oh Billy, you're such an energetic young lad."

The wife motioned towards the kitchen. "Agent, want to have a seat in the kitchen? The cookies are cooling on a rack on the counter."

Mal had that creepy vibe crawling along his spine. This family was far too cheery to have some psycho hacker child. Plus, they were living in the '50s; he couldn't see the older child even owning a computer, or at least one capable of going onto the Internet.

"Sure, I don't see the harm in that." Mal followed the mom to the kitchen as he continued his small talk. "Is Ned home?"

The dad, who took up the rear, replied. "Not at the moment, he went to the corner store to pick up a quart of milk for the cookies. Neddy likes cookies and milk."

The mom smiled as she added. "Don't we all honey?"

"You're darn tootin' right dear."

Mal felt incredibly awkward as he took a seat. The dad took the chair across from him. The mom brought the cookie plate over and offered one to Mal. He didn't want to be rude and accepted the sweet gesture.

The overly happy dad just kept staring at the strange agent. "She makes the best cookies; wins every year at the town fair. Don't you dear?"

Mal smiled as he bit into the cookie. It was dry and tasted terrible. But he chewed through the tough cookie and found it hard to even swallow, but he did. "Yeah, the best I've ever had." He took another bite. Both the mom and dad just watched as Mal ate the entire cookie. Once he finished, he asked again. "So, when will Ned be back?"

The two parents stared in silence as their grins erected more. It was creepy how happy these two were. And Mal found out why. His powers slowly began to fade until they were gone. Shocked, he did his best to remain completely calm as he tried to recall how... then it hit him, the cookie.

"Is there something wrong Mister Agent?" The dad, seemingly all innocent, asked.

In eye-wide shock, Mal exclaimed. "What was in that cookie?"

"Everything you would normally find in your basic cookie recipe with a touch of that serum that negates a Supers power." Mal shot up from his chair, knocking it over. He couldn't believe these two old people got the better of him. He stormed for the front door, but the father blocked his way.

Mal knew the dad was no match, even without his powers. He went to shove the man out of his way, but couldn't budge him. The dad then grabbed his wrist and effortlessly twisted it. His strength was amazing, just by squeezing it, the dad was able to bring Mal down to a knee.

Desperate and in pain, Mal searched for an option. He was close enough to the kitchen counter and grabbed one of the knives. He took the blade and drove it straight into the dad's chest. Thinking it would kill him, Mal watched as the dad looked down at the blade and reply.

"Why would you wreck such a fancy and classy housecoat?" He then used his free hand to grab Mal by the throat and begin to slowly choke the life within.

The dad's voice changes and another person asked through him. "Who are you really and what do you want?"

Choking and coughing, Mal struggled to ask, "Neddy?"

A furious tone replied. "I really, really hate that name!"

● ● ●

No response, no new leads, this day isn't turning out to be the memorable day I had in mind. How was I going to track Peterson down when he seems to be one step ahead of me? Was this worth losing my family and job? If it all pans out, then yes. I just wish it didn't have to come to that. But you got to do what is needed for the greater good sometimes.

One thing did strike my interest on the Net; a teen has been glorifying his success of the super being project. He proclaimed to have perfected it and has been toying with the idea of injecting himself to grant "cool awesome abilities." If this is true and after what happened at Gary's, I can only presume Chronos will be sending their goon squad to retrieve his data. This is my moment, if I could get to him first and take the data, I could use it to help me in finding Peterson. But I had to be careful, I was no match for most of the goons working for Chronos, even with my father's ring. So recon work and track the data might be the better way.

The drive to the address I found where Ned Carver resided was boring and silent since my radio didn't seem to work. I parked a few spaces down the road and just kept a watch. I wanted to see what I was possibly getting myself into before just running in. Only an idiot would just walk up and knock on the door of a suspect that stole classified data that could grant you Superpowers.

After all, he was a sixteen-year-old boy, probably a nerd and loner in school, perhaps an only child. And going through his teens probably hates his parents too. My best guess, he's living in the basement, on the computer, most of the time was sucking back on energy drinks to keep him up.

Plus, I'm not here for him per se, I'm more curious as to who Chronos will send to get him. I'm crossing my fingers that they send Mav; then I can finally get some face to face with him and see if he even got my letter.

I didn't have to wait long. A man in dark clothes wearing sunglasses strolled his way up to the front door. I could tell instantly he wasn't with the SBU; must mean he's from Chronos. Just my luck, it's not Maverine. But I don't recognize him. A new recruit perhaps? A new recruit could mean he's not corrupted yet like the others. He could be my new way into Chronos.

I watched as the door opened, standing inside looked like the mom. Did he just enter the home? Who was this rookie? I waited for the door to close and sneak my way over. I peeked through the window while hiding in the shrub. I must say, they do take really nice care of their lawn and bush, I might need them to come to my place and spruce up my lawn, all I have is weeds and dead grass.

The dad was in his housecoat, their youngest in the living room. Something just wasn't right with this scenario. It was a Wednesday; the dad's home from work and the kids aren't in school? Just great, they're moving to the back of the house now, I wonder what's back there.

I kept my head down as I scurried to the rear of the house. I had to get up on my tippy-toes to see through the kitchen window. What the heck, the Chronos agent is down on one knee; the dad has a knife in his chest and holding him by the throat. What was my red flag? There was a gushing of blood from the knife wound.

I drew my pistol and barged in through the back door.

• • •

After shouting the commanding words, "Police, don't move!" the mom lunged for the gun. Her strength was remarkable for a petite lady, but Pongo accidentally pulled back on the trigger. The bullet struck her in the forehead and after hearing a lead bullet strike metal; Pongo knew for certain, she wasn't human.

Her synthetic skin singed, you could now see the metal skull that was underneath. Ma and Pa were not human. Mal saw this too as the dad tossed him down the hallway, back towards the front. The dad made a charge for Pongo who now knew they weren't human and wasn't going to hesitate to shoot. After emptying half a pistol clip into Pa and having no results, the robot backhanded his intruder, sending him across the kitchen.

Alone with two nonhuman attackers, Pongo had no choice but to slip on the ring.

Meanwhile still powerless, Mal leaned up, collected his thoughts, and saw the young boy standing in the living room, staring right at him. As he slowly got to his feet, Billy ran at him full tilt and tackled him. The boy wasn't human either; he too was incredibly strong and heavy for his size. Mal could feel the effects of the cookie starting to fade now.

The boy sat on Mallarian's chest and began to choke the life from him. Mal, hoping some of his powers returned, held out his hands and unleashed a smaller than usual blast. His normal blast was nowhere near the power of the Kids, but it did the job when needed. The force was enough to push the boy off and but barely left a scorch mark.

He stretched his arm out and reached inside his pocket room, looking for his blade. When he found it, he pulled it out just as the boy made a diving attack. With one swift swing, Mal decapitated the head of the boy and watched as the dismembered head roll away; sparking and fizzing the whole time. That definitely confirmed it, the family were robots of some sort.

Pongo held out his fist, aiming the ring directly at his two attackers. He heard Mal holler from the hall, "They're robots or something, definitely not human!" but Pongo already figured that out. A massive fist appeared and grabbed the dad and without effort, removed his head from the neck.

The mom went to attack, but an attack from behind that sliced off her head prevented that.

Both men were standing over two headless bodies and no sign of the Hacker.

Both sticking their hands at one another, to anyone watching, not very intimidating, but if you knew what those hands were capable of, it was. Suspicious of Pongo, Mal was the first to break the hostile silence.

"Not that I'm not grateful pal that you charged in and saved the day, but who are you?"

Pongo not wanting to back down since he didn't know this guy, did. He dropped his arms and removed the ring, figuring it would get the ball rolling smoother and hopefully, faster. "I'm Eric Pongo, formerly with the SBU."

Mal didn't like what he heard, after his day, the experience he's had with the SBU... but this guy was different than the rest, he helped him. And he did say former. "Go on."

"I'm here looking for the Hacker."

"You and me both pal. I get him first and you can have what's left, sound good?"

Pongo nodded and shook his hand. "Just one more question, who are you working for?"

"An undisclosed government company," Mal remembered the voice on the dad robot and changed the subject. He noticed the not so well hidden camera up in the corner of the room. In a whisper, he told Pongo. "I think he's watching us." He used his eyes to move towards the camera.

Pongo caught on. "I see, where would you be if you were sixteen, a loner hacker and living with your fake parents?"

"Cooped up in the basement in front of my computer most likely," Mal caught on and did his best to look for the door leading to the basement without looking like he was. If Ned was watching, he didn't want to alert him.

The door was in the hallway just outside of the kitchen. As Pongo reached for the knob, someone from the other side opened it first. A beautiful young brunette in a skimpy lacy teddy was standing there, looking sweet and innocent. She giggled when she saw them and had a bubbly, valley girl speech when she greeted them. "Like hi, are you here to see my Neddy?"

Confused, but not willing to harm an innocent girl, Mal replied. "Yeah is he downstairs?"

"He totally doesn't like uninvited visitors and such." She had in her hand, a disk and handed it to Mal. "He says this is what you came for, now leave."

Mal took the disk and pocketed it. But he and Pongo weren't going anywhere. "Listen, Miss," he gently grabbed her by the shoulder and motioned for her to step aside as he continued. "We're not leaving without Ned. So step aside and let us down. We don't want to harm you."

While twirling her long curly hair, she playfully said. "You won't hurt little old me, will you?"

Shaking his head, Mal reassured her as he pulled her out of the doorway. Her smile flipped right around as an angered young teen wrenched Mal's arm, put him in a painful arm hold, and with great strength, shoved him into Pongo.

On the ground, on top of one another, Pongo shoved the man off him and stated the obvious. "She's a damn love-bot." And he drew his pistol, emptying the rest of the clip.

The bullets harmlessly bounced off her metallic interior, but the force of each bullet kept her at bay. That allowed Mal to act, pulling his sword out and delivering the fatal swing at her neck. Both men stormed the basement to find it had been recently abandoned.

Making small talk and keeping a watch out for more surprises, Pongo mentioned. "You know you can't take that disk back to Chronos right? They're not who you think they are."

"Oh what, let me guess, you want it for yourself, is that it? Or you're here to collect it for you boss, or put it up on auction online to the highest bidder?"

"You're way over your head here, that's all. I'm not the bad guy here, I'm..."

Mal cut in, "You're part of the SBU. Biased humans who hunt down Supers; I read the news."

"I said former agent, I've not affiliated with them anymore. Besides Chronos is far worse than anything I've seen in the SBU. Peterson is one sick twisted person. Do you know why you're bringing in Supers?"

"To help them understand their power and if they are a threat to the city, we put them in isolation. Like what the SBU does, but more efficient."

"I can't believe this; newsflash pal you've been brainwashed." Pongo chuckled as he recalled something long ago. They just managed to reach the bottom of the steps. "Reminds me of this time Kyle was able to talk his way through..."

"Did you say, Kyle? He's the one who hands me my missions."

Pongo's jaw dropped, it made sense now. He muttered to himself. "That's what happened to him. But did he turn or does Peterson have something on him?"

The basement was a pigsty, he had multiple computers networked together, hundreds of gaming paraphernalia, a heart pillow bed in the corner, and countless empty energy cans tossed all around. The monitors lit up and on it was a recording of Ned, laughing maniacally, taunting them. "You can't catch me, na-na-na! Nice attempt boys; that disk I gave you does in fact contain the data Chronos wanted back. I kept a copy for myself and no, you won't be able to access it on my computer. I hope your boss enjoys the tweaking I did with the data. But that depends on if you douche-bags can make it out in time. You have about ten seconds left before... well you know. So long and until next time, you're a bunch of noobs."

Eye-wide in shock, both men knew the place was about to blow. So they scrambled up the stairs and ran for the exit. Mallarian took to the air and flew through the living room window while Pongo quickly placed the ring on, formed the armor, and flew out the back just in the nick of time. Once clear, the house exploded, leaving nothing left.

SUPERS: MALLARIAN PART 2

Once again Mallarian found himself inside the elevator of the Chronos building empty-handed. Well, he did get the disk but was still unsure of what to do with it. Was this Pongo fellow right, was Chronos the evil ones? But could he go against the people who gave him a second chance at life? Did that warrant the right to hand over the disc? Until Mal knew for certain, he reached into his abyss, stashed the disc in there, and had the gateway to it closed just as the doors parted.

Standing there talking to a techie, Kyle was looking deeply concerned. But when he saw Mal coming off the elevator, that worry disappeared. But returned when he saw the empty hands and dissatisfied look on the man's face.

"I take it the Hacker's place didn't go smoothly?"

Mal didn't know what to say and just went with his what his gut said. "Sorry, maybe I'm not cut out for this stuff. Let me tell you though, Ned was prepared for us. He knew we would become. The sick bastard replaced his family with robots. I didn't even know you could make robots, did you?"

Kyle paused, that slight hesitation gave Mal his answer. Kyle's verbal answer was, "No."

"In the middle of the battle, the kid must have fled and rigged his computer stuff to blow. I just barely got out of there." Mal wasn't sure if he should share everything that happened, in particular, the ex-agent of the SBU. He decided to go "fishing" to see if he could get some kind of reaction from Kyle.

"There was a mystery guy there; he was helping me fight the robot family. He said he was a former agent of the SBU..." That there grabbed Kyle's attention, it was like he knew the name before Mal said it. "Said his name was, Peter, Pan, Panda, no, Pongo, that's right? Does that name ring a bell."

Kyle checked over his shoulder, like someone may be listening. He shook his head and replied. "Not really, but a former agent you say? Perhaps he's gone rogue and was seeking the data for personal gain. Did you get a chance to talk to him?"

"We didn't really talk, just exchanged names and flashed our BS credentials. I lost sight of him during the explosion; not sure he made it out."

Kyle seemed to be upset, even about to shed a tear. But kept his composure. "Well good, one less guy interfering with our business." He then remembered the tablet in his hands and brought Mal's attention to it. "Speaking of business; I have another mission for you. I sent Superbat and Bryan to retrieve a fresh Super. That was right around the time you left and I haven't heard back from them. The techies were able to trace Bryan's cell phone and via satellite imagery spotted him. This is a live feed..."

Mal looked at the screen and saw the speedster racing across the Atlantic Ocean. That was odd in itself. "Where's he going? You know he's too fast for me to catch him."

Kyle nodded. "He's not answering his phone. But we don't need to catch him, just locate Superbat and find out what went wrong." Kyle walked Mal back to his office. Inside he approached his desk and picked up a folder. "Here's the mission I sent them on. I'd get you some backup, but everyone else is out on other assignments." Kyle stressed the next part so it was clear. "I don't want you being a hero here. Something isn't right. Bryan and Superbat are two of the best. So I just want you to figure out what happened to them and bring them back."

Holding the file Mal asked, "And what about the subject?"

For the first time today, Kyle hesitated. Mal didn't know why. Kyle plainly said. "When you find our men, complete the mission together." He reached for a notepad and pen and scribbled something down. "Now if you'll excuse me mister Mallarian, I have other endeavors that need my attention. Is there anything else?"

Mal had his orders and file. When he couldn't think of anything he just shook his head. Kyle politely motioned for the door and extended his hand. "Well, good luck. Bring our comrades home safely."

Slightly confused by the gesture, Kyle never shook his hand before, except for the first time they met, Mal took it. Kyle very crafty man that he is folded the paper and using a sleight of hand, slipped the note between Mal's fingers. He could read Kyle's eyes, they said don't say a word, just turn around and go about your mission. So Mal did just that.

Outside, away from the building on another rooftop, Mal took a moment to read over the secret note. It read: Do not bring the subject back to Chronos, locate Pongo, he's alive. That got Mal thinking.

Well, Kyle lied, after all, he knew the former agent. But why was Kyle telling him one thing, and on a note, passed in secret, another; unless his office and the whole building is bugged.

"What the heck is going on?" Mal asked himself. And how did he know if he survived or not?

He opened the folder to reveal an image of a boy, maybe around eight years of age. That was troubling in itself. It's one thing to track down Supers who are on the run, or a potential danger to society, but kidnapping a child, that's crossing the line. How dangerous can one child be? Not much else was in the file, the boy's address and name; Brett Mitchell.

Kyle had interviewed the teachers at his school, learned the child was having difficulties focusing. Also, the strange, unexplainable phenomenon began happening around the school and at home. It wasn't hard for Kyle to put the pieces together. It still didn't explain what this kid could do.

But one thing Mal had to do, find Superbat and get some facts. So he took to the air and headed for the address given.

• • •

I watched as the dust and debris settled but saw no sign of the man working for Chronos. Even worse, he has the Hacker's backup disk and was going to bring it back to Chronos. That didn't belong back with Peterson, we erased his files for a reason and now all is for nothing. But I found myself alone, with no leads or help. Maybe I should admit defeat.

Suddenly I felt my phone vibrate, curious I pulled it out and noticed I had an email. Fingers crossed, maybe he finally got back to me. But it wasn't, it was from someone by the name, "Lady-Charmer." Just great, probably some spam porno junk mail.

I went to delete it, but something stopped me. The subject line read: get your man in time. The word Chronos is often portrayed as an old man who goes by the name "Father Time." I clicked the email open and I knew I made the right choice. It was an address in the city, not too far from where I am now. It suddenly dawned on me, the name from which the email came from. It must mean Kyle was still my mole and he must be a prisoner inside the building.

I know I can't rescue Kyle. But if he wanted out, he wouldn't have an issue leaving. He must have a reason to stick around and once I get to this address and do whatever he needs me to do, I'm sure I'll have my answer. I've seen that man do a lot of crazy things with that ability of his, he could sell ice to an Eskimo without even batting an eye.

But I wonder what was at this address for me. Whatever it is, hopefully, it's what we need to bring Peterson down. This day wasn't going according to exactly as planned, but the address wasn't far, so I ran back to my car.

• • •

Mal landed in the bushes of the neighborhood park and approached the house on foot. Doing his best to be inconspicuous, he calmly walked down the sidewalk towards the targeted house. He noticed up ahead, in a tree, a familiar unconscious man. It was Superbat but in his human form.

Mal floated up and brought the man down to the ground. He took a little pleasure slapping the man in the face to wake him up. It worked, Superbat jolted forward, sweat forming from his brow. He saw where he was and Mal there; he was completely confused.

He even managed to blurt out, "Who, what, huh?"

"You tell me. Where's Bryan; what happened to him?"

Superbat shook the cobwebs in his head and took a deep breath. He did his best to explain. "We were on assignment, to get this kid. Bryan and I didn't have any issues with it, even though Kyle seemed to hesitate. It's the job; it's what we get paid for I say. Anyways, Bryan said, since he was young, his parents were probably frightened of the crazy things that have been happening; we figured we approach it like we were consultants here to just talk to the boy. And when we got in, nab him. If the parents resisted, take care of them."

Take care of them? That didn't sit well with Mal, but brushed it off and allowed Superbat to continue.

"So we went to the front door, Bryan rang the bell, the door opened and that's when I heard Bryan scream like a little girl. He was so damn scared of something, I couldn't see what; he bolted off. Before I could say anything, it was like I was thrown into the air and the next thing I remember is waking up here."

What was this kid? More importantly, should he join up with the Bat and Bryan who seem determined to bring him back? Should he listen to Kyle's message, what would happen if he didn't bring this one back? He'd make enemies with Chronos no doubt, especially if he had to fight these two off to save the kid. Nothing was clear here, except for who exactly was this kid and what did Chronos want with him?

Mal looked down the road and saw an old beat-up sedan park a few houses down from the address in question. Using his superb vision he was able to bypass the glare of the windshield and see that former agent Pongo fellow. Was it a coincidence or did Kyle tip him off too?

He knew he had to lose the Bat before approaching Pongo. "Hey, why don't you head back and get a check-up, I'll head off and look for Bryan."

Superbat nodded, he did feel queasy, but then remembered the mission. "What about the kid?"

"Hey, if he took the two of you out without even seeing you, I say we hold off; gather some more before walking back into the unknown. Wouldn't you agree?"

The bat nodded and smiled. "Yeah, you're right. I'll head back and grab the others."

Mallarian was impressed by how easy it was to get rid of him. Maybe Kyle was rubbing off on him. Knowing he was short on time since,

Bryan the speedster could zoom in at any moment, not to mention, if the Bat manages to grab Sue, they could just appear, he ran over to the driver's side of the sedan.

A confused and cautious Pongo rolled the window down and asked. "How may I help you? I see you survived the blast."

Mal didn't want to bother with the small talk, he wanted answers. He just handed Pongo the note and folder given to him by Kyle. The former agent skimmed through it, as his eyes widened. "Well, I'll be dammed."

Frustrated, Mallarian shouted. "Will someone actually share some information with me?"

Pongo explained. "As you know, Chronos can create their own Supers. Peterson, the CEO of Chronos has been trying to perfect it for many years. For what and why is still unclear. But he's also been looking for a psychic; there are extremely rare. Venkman, the leader of the City's Hero group is the only one known. And he's quite powerful. As for why you'll have to ask your boss. So I presume this kid is a psychic, from what I gather glancing over your folder. Why else would Chronos risk bringing in a child Super for?"

That didn't answer many of the questions Mal was thinking, it really only raised more. "And what's this got to do with Kyle?"

"Kyle's just one of his tools, because of his remarkable gift of persuasion. He can make people do immoral things just by asking."

Well, that explains to Mal why he was doing things he normally wouldn't. "How do you two know each other?"

"When I was with the SBU, I caught up with the infamous conman. This was early on in my career. As I was arresting him, he took one look at me and said, "You don't want to do this, you want to let me go and forget about me." And I did. Luckily, I had written the encounter down or I would have forgotten. Later I got smart..."

Mal interrupted; after all, the clock was ticking. "Save it for another day. We need to get this kid before the others come back."

"Who's coming back?"

"Bryan the speedster, the Superbat fellow, probably that Kid..."

Pongo knew they were no match. Not many are. And who knows, if Peterson desperately wants this child, he will send everyone. They were going to need help, Super help. It was time to call in all the big guns.

But there was one question that was still fuzzy to Pongo. Who was Mallarian and where did he stand? He asked. "But before we go further, I need to know one thing; who are you? Are you one of the good guys or just in it for the money?"

Mallarian stepped back, he too was unsure of who he was now. He was given a second chance at life. He swore if he lived through that tragic day he'd change his life around, become a better person. Was this that moment to redeem all those things he's done in the past?

It was obvious; Mallarian wasn't his real first name or his last. It was a name he used to use as an alias, whether it was online chat rooms, video games, that world knew him only by that name. So when Kyle and Peterson confronted him in the hospital, lying there almost dead, and offered the chance to live once again and with Superpowers, Frank LeMayes couldn't refuse. But now as he looked back, was he forced to agree by Kyle, or did he do it willingly?

Before the accident Frank was kind of an honest criminal; well he would say so. He only stole from those who could afford it or had insurance to be properly reimbursed. He never killed anyone, harmed and injured, yes, but when he was forced to. All his life he was put down, had nothing, his parents died when he was young, and had no other relatives willing to take him in. That meant two options; foster care or a life on the streets. He tried both.

But Frank drew the straw when he teamed up with Stan Sparks, a professional thief. Stan had planned a bank heist and needed extra hands. But it didn't go as thought; after Stan shot down two of the guards and a hostage, the SBU had no choice but to act. At that time, the City's Heroes were still new, and the hatred the SBU had for them was at its strongest. They felt they had to prove to the people, they didn't need Supers to help them protect the city.

But when they heard that the Junker and Venkman were on their way, they acted fast. Headstrong, they raided the bank, lost some more hostages but brought down the criminals. Frank was lying there, on the brink of death as the paramedics brought him to the hospital. He wasn't sure what happened to the other two.

The doctors couldn't do anything but watch Frankie suffer; the bullet was too close to his heart. They left him alone since he had no one to visit except for two men, Mister Peterson and his liaison Kyle. They offered to help Frankie, give him another possible chance at life. The Super Being experiment was only successful once before. Frankie was dying anyway, so he had nothing to lose.

Mallarian looked Pongo dead in the eyes and nodded; knowing he just betrayed the company that gave him a second chance at life. But that second chance wasn't going to be to follow the same path as before. With this Super change, he was going to do right with it.

Pongo smiled. "Let's help this child. Hopefully, we can be convincing enough for them to let us help."

SUPERS: PETERSON

This is a recording for Charles E. Peterson's personal files: Earth date March 30th, 2015.

I'm recording this for historic reasons, I want this as a memo of what I have managed to accomplish. And in case I do not live tomorrow, people will understand my story, and one day, a worthy successor will continue what I have started.

Ninety-nine times; that's how many times I and others have tried to kill me over the years. I personally have tried every way I could think of. How old am I? Good question, it's been so long I can't recall. If I were to guess, I say a few hundred years. Was I the very first special person? Not even close, there have been many others; although nothing quite to the power scale as I have been seeing as of late. Even though I'm immortal, I've always been envious of what other Supers could do. Like way back when I was with the SBU and met fellow Supers like this Maverine, and Wolfganger and after hearing Maverine talk about the nearby future, a most brilliant idea came to mind.

You see most of these Supers just use their powers for their personal gain. Nothing but greedy selfish adolescents on a quest for lust and gluttony. If I had their gifts, I would do so much. I would protect these pathetic vermin and force them to bow down and proclaim myself as their new God. A dream that someday I will achieve, after all, I do have time on my hands.

Working alongside some of them has only made my lust for their power greater; especially the one, Ami Marik. She possesses the ability to mimic another Super's powers just by touching them. I want her power, but she whines and goes on about how excruciatingly painful the process is for her if she decides to keep the power permanently. Live the life I have sweetie and then you'll know to suffer. Where were you during the dark ages? When the black plague blanketed these lands, the disease slowly ate away at the sick and hungry. Plus, everywhere I went since I was immortal, I couldn't be killed; they saw me as a witch, a demon worshiper, and ran me out of town. Those were days worth bitching about, not gaining an infinite amount of abilities to use whenever desired.

That got me thinking, this new world, science isn't the Devil's work; it is looked at like a miracle. I could give myself powers, like Ami, and have what I've always craved; ultimate power. But I needed funding and more importantly, test rats because there will be many trials and errors, and I rather not be an error.

It took many years to build up the resources needed to fund my new project. When the idea was looking grim, about to give up all hope, I came across triplet geniuses who collectively figured it out. But it needs the blood of my former colleague Miss Marik. Only a drop of it is crucial to the success of the procedure; basically, it is the essential key to it all.

So I sent my personal bodyguard, Agentman, to retrieve as much blood from Miss Marik as it'll take. Agentman has been very loyal, money, and promises I don't intend to keep can persuade anybody. I am just fortunate enough that has a unique set of skills to make it worth my time; hmm I'll have to acquire them when everything is good to go.

But regretfully, there have been a few bumps along this road; one in particular, SBU agent Eric Pongo has been asking too many questions and sticking his nose in my business. I sent one of my loyal men to take care of him.

Then I'm told I need the blood of a pure Super to duplicate the power I want. Well, my company already has Supers doing government tasks, why can't I have them gather "hostile" Supers as well? At first, getting them to do immoral tasks without question was difficult. But then I got a gift as Kyle dropped onto my lap. Sure, I had to kidnap his family to force him to work for me; he wouldn't accept money, what's a guy to do?

Let's discuss my glitches on the road, shall we?

I was hesitant to see that Maverine enlisted. At first, I kept a watchful eye and didn't want to give him missions crucial to my plan. I still don't trust the man, no one should. He, for as long as I've known him, has been in it for himself.

Pongo was working with Gadgetman and had him steal my super being data and tossed into our systems an encrypted virus that erased all of the data; leaving us in the dark and bringing my plan to a sudden halt. This was an outrage, I ordered Kyle to get our newest recruit to retrieve it immediately. I know what you are thinking, why would you ever send the fresh meat on such a daunting task. Mallarian is the best suited. You see, we injected many powers into him and Kyle ensured me he could. Plus it's been a very hectic day.

But it wasn't a total loss. We discovered that the alias "The Hacker" a month ago now, had copied the data and our techies finally were able to triangulate and discover his whereabouts. I ordered Kyle to send in the troops and retrieve said data. Once again, mission unsuccessful. I find out that he sent the same fool that botched the first mission; why would he do that?

I have men searching the globe, looking for any possible leads as to maybe; just maybe this Hacker kid shared the data with someone else. But I tripled the scientist personnel and they are working nonstop, reviewing the papers we have on hand. I'm remaining hopeful that they will figure it out, for their families' sakes.

Today should be the day everyone remembers; because tomorrow should be the day they will be bowing down to me, their new God.

If someone else is listening to this, I guess I didn't make it through number one-hundred and hope you will finish what I started.

Fingers are crossed.

On a personal note, when I do become God, I think I will change the name again. Charles E. Peterson is getting rather dull; you can only keep a name for so long.

● ● ●

Three well-suited men walked into the office of the CEO who just finished his recording. He was behind his desk, cutting the tip of a Cuban rolled cigar. With a strike of the wooden match, he sucked back that intoxicating taste before addressing his guests.

"Where are we with Miss Marik's blood Agentman?"

The three men talked in unison when they answered. "We have sent two of our people out on the assignment. The security there is tight with the severe rising of Supers and the strange occurrences popping up around the city. But we have full confidence we will have it in time."

Peterson seemed somewhat irritated as he waved the men to stop. "Please, I can't stand when there are multiple of your present. The extra chatter isn't necessary." The three nodded as the two on either end oozed away and blended into the middle.

After he slowly exhaled the toxic fumes, he asked. "What about the other hitch in the plan?"

"We instructed Kyle to give him a mission and we have set up a trap for him. In an hour, Maverine will be dead."

"Excellent, that will force Venkman to act. And cloud his judgment in a rage to track down his killer. A distraction I'm hoping to capitalize on. Now, when you exit, will you let Kyle know that I will see him now, he's not cooperating with the deal."

"Would you prefer if we leave a few during your meeting?"

Peterson let out a wicked grin. "Station two just outside. I don't fear his charming persuasion, he knows what I will do if he tries to defile me."

Agentman bowed before he left and barely a minute after his departure, Kyle gave a gentle knock before entering. A grinning Peterson welcomed him in and offered a seat, but Kyle preferred to stand. He didn't want to waste time.

"What is it now... Sir? As you're well aware, we're crazy busy today and I thought you wanted results, pronto is the word you used wasn't it?"

"Don't play mind games with me; remember who you are speaking to." He leaned back on the chair and stroked his clean-shaven chin. "I want to know why you haven't been able to retrieve the super being data yet. I gave you ample choices and leads."

Kyle just shrugged his shoulders. "Hey, you made and recruited these failures, not me. The deal was that I hand out the missions and help them in they seem hesitant. But there are many Supers locked up in quarantine, siphoning their blood and as to the recovery of the data..." Kyle paused for a moment. "What can I say? I sent the best choice..."

Peterson burst out into uncontrollable laughter, "The best choice? Maverine or even Bryan would be the top choice. Not fresh meat. He was supposed to hunt down Supers, that's why I gave him a particular set of abilities..."

Kyle cut in, "No, you wanted to see how many abilities a single being could sustain, no care what might happen to the subject."

Peterson dabbed the ashes from his cigar. "Relax, I told Doctor Wells to give him a reduced power level on them. We gave him minor versions of the powers we currently had on file. Wells is just a nervous Nancy. I have full faith in the results."

Kyle used good excuses to mask what he was doing. "He's unstable and Dr. Wells did stress that many abilities shoved into one specimen could be catastrophic. Maybe that's why he's failing, his body and mind are losing touch with themselves."

Peterson didn't care and continued with his initial concerns. "With this apprehension of yours, not to mention he failed miserably the first time, why did you allow a second attempt? Hell, he's only performed one task successfully hasn't he? If he's not performing, he's expendable."

Kyle nodded and explained. "And that's exactly why I sent him after the Wolf sir, and have given Maverine plenty of breadcrumbs that will lead him to Mallarian. He wants blood for the person who murdered his buddy. Get him to eliminate the failure."

Peterson slid a folder note across the table. "Excellent, send him to this address. Tell him that's where the man who murdered the Wolf is hiding."

Kyle was frustrated; he wanted to end Peterson right there but he restrained himself and took a deep breath before asking. "And when can I see my family? When is my job here done? I've done some things I'm not proud of in my day, but this is getting to me. Please, I beg you, they are innocent."

Peterson let out a wicked grin when he replied. He knew they were the only reason Kyle was here and if he knew where they were, he'd lose his leverage. Kyle would just walk out and get them back. "Didn't you read your contract before signing? You are in this for the long haul my dear friend."

"I'm not your friend. And I have a line and you're walking very close to it." Tears began to pool around Kyle's eyes when he continued. "Don't get me wrong Mister Peterson, I love my family. But even they wouldn't want me to be doing what I am for their safety. Don't cross that line, I won't hesitate again."

Peterson didn't show his emotions, he was cold when he leaned forward and exhaled. "Trust me; your work here is almost complete. Soon I'll have everything I need. Now get me that data, send Maverine to those coordinates, and get this for me..." He tossed a folder across the table. Kyle picked it up and opened it. There was a picture of a young boy, his name Brett Mitchell.

"You want this boy? He's merely a child; I can't..."

"If you do this, I'll set your family free. However, you serve the remainder of your time before you see them. Now go, get back what is mine and no more failures, and if this new Mallarian character botches another mission; dispose of him. We don't have time for failure or a weak link."

Kyle nodded and left.

SUPERS: TREE

Pongo and Mal stood impatiently in the waiting room several floors above the Heroes headquarters that was thirty floors above the City Hall district, it was the tallest building in the city and literally in the middle of the ever-growing town. The Heroes facility took up fifteen floors of the building; most of it was research labs and fighting/practicing areas for new members to train

The Heroes had to be up high, so they could look down upon the city and have the edge. The only other building to come close to its height was the SBU main quarters, but it was closer to the water, looking out towards the Island.

The receptionist informed them that Tree, the second in command, would be with them shortly.

The oversized door slid open and standing on the opposite side was an eight-foot-tall hulking humanoid Tree dressed in a tailored-fit lab coat. His arms were thick branches, his "hair" just twigs and leaves. His Super name was Tree, not very clever, but he was a man of science.

Doctor Bill Grunsom was a world-renowned biologist who was working with the late Doctor Wynona Wells. They were working for Chronos a year back, trying to splice the Supers genes with plants and animals.

One late night, Bill was working alone, there was a robbery that went wrong, an explosion erupted and the plant specimen's DNA spilled and entered the mouth of an unconscious Doctor. His body transformed overnight and when he woke up, he was what he is today; unable to transform out of it.

He fled Chronos and was on the run until Venkman brought him in. Tree is incredibly strong, tough bark skin, and rapidly heals in the sunlight.

He was polite when he addressed the strangers, well, only the one was. He knew who Pongo was. "Former agent Eric Pongo," You could see somewhat of a smile through that bark skin. "A pleasure as always; I understand you wished to speak with Venkman but I regret to inform you he is unavailable at the moment."

"Please, we need your help. All of you."

Tree was deeply concerned but was hesitant to comply. Mal couldn't figure out why that was, after all, these were the City's Heroes, helping is what they do.

Tree explained. "Mister Pongo please, Venkman has already told you. Without some proof, we can't get involved. Chronos, like the SBU and us, are government-affiliated and don't investigate one another. They're watching our every move. If we start an illegal investigation... well, you know what will happen. But even worse for us since we're Supers. They'll lock us up on the island.

But besides, we're incredibly busy with everyday crime. The Junker and White Light are working day and night just to keep up. Venkman is out of town, the Chameleon is on a special mission that I can't disclose. I'm on backup duty for the others. Without enough evidence, we just don't have the manpower to aid you. But if you found some strong evidence, I could take it to Venkman and see what he says..."

Pongo shoved the folder Mal had into his branchy arms. "Read this; Peterson wants this child, a psychic child. We both know for what and why." Pongo sensed the lack of concern in Tree's eyes; he couldn't blame him though, this wasn't the first time he came to them for help against Chronos. He has been in this same room and hero before; back before his family was murdered, when he initially dug too close into Peterson's diabolical dealings.

• • •

In the bathroom attached to Kyle's office, the charming man stared in shame at his reflection in the mirror. Shaking his distraught head, trying to find the immoral compass that he wishes laid inside. He couldn't do it; he couldn't use his gifts to persuade a man to bring the child in knowing what the scientists were going to do with him. But if he didn't do this, he'd condemn his family to a life of suffering. Peterson wouldn't just have them killed; he'd want to slowly enjoy watching Kyle suffer.

Kyle had the ultimate choice to make. After splashing some water on his face and patting it dry with the soft fluffy towel, he went to leave but heard a whisper coming from above. He looked up and saw nothing but the tile ceiling; until he looked closer. There, blending with the background, a familiar figure stared right back at him.

Hanging from the ceiling the Chameleon whispered. "That's a right old friend. I've been watching you like a fly on the wall."

Surprised, intrigued, and wondering why someone was stuck to his bathroom ceiling, Kyle replied. "Nick, how long have you been watching me?"

"Don't keep staring up, you'll raise suspicion; and second, it's Chameleon now. Pretend to pee or something will ya?"

Kyle turned his head and continued to pat his face dry. "Have you been watching me pee?"

The Chameleon spoke in whispers. "Let's not worry about the small details and get to the real point of my intrusion. Pongo came to us a while back, Venkman sent me in to make contact with you since all this strange crap started happening. It took some time to get in here; I'm impressed, Chronos updated their security since I hacked in last time. I assume you're Pongo's, inside man?"

"Why else would I be stuck in here against my will?"

"Umm, can't you just talk your way out?"

"Peterson has my family somewhere else. I'm assuming at another secret location; there's an underground facility somewhere in the city. I'm just not sure where. I can't find the schematics for it."

"Hey, leave that to me. That's what I do."

Kyle addressed more concerning news. "There's a file on my desk, copy it, and get it back to the others; you need to protect that kid at all costs. Oh, tell Venkman that Mav will need his help. I have to send him into a trap." Kyle was done drying his face, adjusted his tie, and asked one more thing. "Is there anything else?"

"Can you leave me a sandwich or something to eat, I'm starving; been slowly sneaking my way here for hours."

• • •

Pongo and Mallarian were back on the street in his sedan parked a few houses down from Brett Mitchell's place. They had no backup and no plan as to how they were going to approach a possible psychic. And with what happened when Superbat and Bryan went up, their hesitation was sound. But Superbat returned with Bryan and the Kid, forcing them to act quickly.

The three Chronos goons marched forward-thinking Brett couldn't stop them all and one of them will be able to subdue him in time. As the Kid blasted the door, Bryan supercharged in, and the Bat swan dove in, hoping all three simultaneous actions would stump the child.

Pongo and Mal hopped out of the car and rushed the Kid from behind. Pongo slipped the ring on and took to the air. Mal didn't hesitate to blast the Kid who grinning from ear to ear as he blasted the house walls with the screaming parents diving for cover inside. Mal had surprised the Kid and since he wasn't expecting an attack, wasn't in his ghost form. The blast was just enough to knock him to the ground and take him out of the fight.

Bryan stormed into Brett's room and wasted no time to snatch him. But he didn't even get close enough as he ran straight into an almost invisible wall of force that surrounded the frightened child. The fast and unexpected impact knocked the speeder out for the moment. Superbat swooped down and he too collided with the miraculous force field and stunned himself.

Pongo landed near Brett who was in tears and barely able to control his spectacular powers. Pongo held up his hands to show he wasn't here to cause harm. "Please, I'm here to help. Those guys are not."

Brett peered deeply into Pongo's eyes, who knew exactly what he was doing since, after all, he knew another powerful Psychic. Once Brett read his mind he knew this man spoke the truth. "Now you must come with me, they'll send more. My friends and I can keep you safe."

Brett nodded and walked into the arms of Pongo. Once he had him in a hug, he flew off and hollered over to Mal to snatch the parents. Once the three goons from Chronos came to, Brett, his family, and the two intruders were long gone.

The Kid grumbled. "Yo dudes, it was that newb who just got hired."

Bryan nodded. "Kyle has some explaining to do."

SUPERS: AGENTMAN

We are one man with many skills, talents, and abilities and loyal to whoever has the money to hire us. We will protect that person until their untimely death, the highest bidder or the funds stop flowing into our bank accounts. We've worked for many people, companies, and even a few governments... One must admit, this job we have with Mister Peterson is the best so far.

Not many others are quite as unique as us; since after all, the fifteen of us are as one. We can separate ourselves from one another to perform separate tasks. Each holding onto our other handy abilities such as alter our physical appearance to replicate an exact reflection of anyone we wish. We have trained with some of the best, making our combat skills, most deadly and efficient.

Another keynote to make about ourselves, except for the original one, we are immune to that toxic negate serum constructed by those SBU scientists. Of course, this vital information is only known to us, and no one else.

Who are we, where did we come from? None of us possess these memories or have long forgotten them because truthfully, they do that matter to us. Money matters; who are we, our name is Agentman, personal bodyguard to one Mister Charles Peterson trained assassin hunting down the ruthless Maverine for the bounty.

We've crossed paths with the Maverine before either of us joined Chronos. We were hunting the man through several countries. We managed to catch up to him down in Mexico and after the bloody entanglement, we lost sight of him but not before he got one of our own.

You see once we lose one, we cannot bring him back. So what was once fifteen is now only fourteen. And after another losing battle with the Maverine, what was fourteen was now only thirteen. Needless to say, we have a lot of built-up rages and seek vengeance; thirteen times more than any other person in this world.

So when we saw that the Maverine joined Chronos, it brought us excitement, knowing we had him exactly where we wanted. But Peterson ordered us to hold off, he wanted to see why the Maverine would enlist his services, knowing the kind of person he was.

Being a group of thirteen, we can perform many missions at the same time. Three of us are stalking Miss Marik as instructed, looking to steal a few vials of her blood. Meanwhile, two are stationed outside Peterson's office, ensuring his safety while the eight of us gather to form our trap, our revenge against the one man we would kill for no price; Maverine.

● ● ●

Maverine showed up at the destination given for his latest mission. Suspicious of the location, in the abandoned warehouse district, he parked his motorcycle a few blocks away. With his trusty duffle bag full of his random weapons and heavy artillery in hand, he strolled on over to the condemned building in question.

After he argued with Kyle, wanting to know The Wolf's murderer, Kyle gave him the information needed to track him down. He warned Kyle that after he found this person, he was going to burn Chronos to the ground. So with his intentions in place, he entered the giant dark building and took a quick look around. Eyeing the skywalks and every inch but no sign of anyone to be seen.

After a few more steps in, he grumbled under his breath. "Hmm, I smell a trap." And then suddenly a bunch of spotlights flickered on, but his protection goggles prevented the light from blinding him.

He hollered out standing tall and impatient. "Ok, now I'm pissed. Who'd they send? Who has the balls to face me? Did you murder Tom too?"

Then a buzzing now came from overhead, curious, Mav looked up to see a giant magnetized slate hovered over, getting the surprise on him. Before he could react, he lost his bag and those protective goggles slipped off from his head; allowing the light to shine brightly into his severely sensitive eyes. He cringed to a knee, trying his best to shield his eyes from the painfully bright light; but the pain became overwhelming, and found that he was now prone for an ambush.

His attacker wasted no time and tossed down a few gas grenades which landed nearby. As they slowly rolled around, out hissed a dark green gas that quickly engulfed the man. Inside was the negate serum that has been transformed into a gaseous form. It caused Maverine to cough and with each breath, the poison seeped deeper inside; shutting down his powerful abilities.

Then from the shadows, out stepped a total of eight clones belonging to the infamous henchman known as Agentman; each carrying either a shotgun or pistol.

In unison, they all spoke with a cold, dark tone. "You've made the wrong choices, no hard feelings."

Wasting little time, they aimed with the barrel directly pointed at the prone target. And in unison they opened fire, emptying the weapons and every bullet penetrating the infamous Maverine.

Now without his abilities, he fell backward and landed hard. The one clone went over and turned off the spotlights while the rest of the agents stood around the dying man. Maverine coughed up some blood as he tried to move, but couldn't.

"You have killed two of us in the past, now we're here to even the score." They each reloaded their weapons and aimed. They wanted to savor this moment while they could.

Mav found himself for the first time, in a long time, staring down the barrel of his demise.

Agentman grinned; the satisfaction of being the only one to ever get the upper hand on the world's most notorious Super fuelled his ego. "You won't regenerate and come back from this. So, we guess this is goodbye..." They all began to chuckle amongst themselves.

After they calmed down, they cocked their guns and went to finish the Maverine off. But suddenly, each of them was thrown back by an invisible force. After flying several feet backward each one struck the warehouse wall with enough force to go straight through it and disappeared soon after.

From the shadows high above, Venkman floated down and landed beside the dying man. "Damn you Maverine, you should have waited for me. When will you learn?" Using his telekinetic ability, he was able to lift him. He used his mental powers to medically diagnose Maverine's internal wounds. "You're not healing, were you injected with the serum?"

Mav coughed up. "They used the gas form." He was determined now and added. "Chronos needs to pay for all of this. But I don't think they're the only ones in play here."

"You think there is someone else in the shadows? Who? And if we're going to raid Chronos, we're going to need you one-hundred percent." He lifted the man into his arms and began to float high into the air, leaving the warehouse. He explained to his brother that he was taking him back to headquarters, where Medik was there sharing information about the company she is also forced to work for.

Venkman nursed his brother all the way back to the City's Heroes headquarters to the landing platform. Already there to help was Tree. He took Maverine using his massive arms and carried him to the medical ward.

Wasting no time, Medik gently placed her hands onto the wounds and closed her eyes. The same holy light as before illuminated her palms and rapidly healed the wounds.

When the external wounds were healed, Medik dropped to a knee. The extensive healing drained her momentarily and couldn't do it anymore.

Watching from the observing room, a puzzled Tree asked Venkman who was right next to him. "Why isn't he healing on his own? What happened out there?"

"Peterson set up a trap for him, his bodyguard Agentman was waiting, dosed him with the negate serum, shut him down, and started an onslaught…" Venkman glared off, taking the focus on what he was staring at. He couldn't believe his abilities were clouded, he should have seen this coming; so why didn't he? He came back to focus and addressed Tree once more. "I don't care about the repercussions, we're getting involved now. Call everyone back from their missions; we need all the help we can get."

"But Sir, Chameleons searching for the underground fortress Kyle says should be there. The White Light and Junker are handling the everyday Supers; we're shorthanded as it is. We just can't stop protecting the city, the people will rally; this isn't the best time to be seeking vengeance…"

"Tree, this isn't vengeance, this is protecting the city, heck, everyone. I've allowed Chronos to operate under the radar long enough. They're killing fellow Supers, who knows what will happen once Peterson completes his diabolical scheme, whatever it may be."

Tree asked, "Not to ask such obvious questions Sir, but you're a Psychic right, can't you meditate into the future and see what happens?"

"My clairvoyance only affects my immediate area and moments before it happens. But that Mitchell child, his potential powers are far greater than mine, perhaps he could." A frustrated Venkman banged his fist and when he did, he accidentally unleashed a telekinetic force that knocked all objects in the room over. "But we let him slip through our fingers. Let's just pray Peterson didn't get to him first."

"I believe that Mister Pongo and that Mal character were able to get to him first. But they are presently on the run and are unable to make contact with them. We have no leads as to their whereabouts; the White Light has been looking into it. They were supposed to make contact with Maverine and Kyle, but I believe they were compromised beforehand."

"Which means Kyle is in severe danger. Is he still inside the Chronos building?" Tree had to think for a moment, but after a nod of his wooden head, Venkman feared the worst. "Ok, we need to hit that building and rescue Kyle."

Tree stepped back from his comrade, "Um, Sir are you serious? Remember I'm not a soldier, I'm a scientist. You don't really think the two of us can just walk into the Chronos building and retrieve Kyle, do you? They have multiple Supers stationed there."

"Three, you mean three, we have Maverine as well. Medik healed him, he should recover shortly." Immediately after saying that, Medik entered the room, the concerned look on her face said it all.

Venkman didn't like reading his friends' minds, but she was too distraught to speak. *Maverine, his abilities don't seem to be returning.*

He inhaled a lot of that serum it seems; I fear they may never… He didn't want to hear anymore and stopped listening in.

Turning to Tree, he informed him. "We're on our own."

Medik went to offer her help but Venkman stopped her before she got out one word.

"No offense, you're a healer, not a fighter. You should stay here and watch over him," He turned to Tree and said the same thing.

Tree stumbled with words; he was dumbfounded that Venkman stated he'll go alone to rescue Kyle.

He went to say something but Medik got her words out first. "Sir, with all due respect, I need to get back now, before they realize I left."

"I understand and thank you for risking coming. I wasn't sure if we were going to need your services but I like to be safe and not sorry."

Tree grabbed Venkman's arm, preventing him from storming out to go headstrong into a building armed with an unknown amount of Supers. "Why don't you go track *her* down? See if she's willing to help us out here."

"Last I heard she willingly joined Chronos…"

Tree did his best to explain or hypothesize the situation. "She's not like that; I believe she only joined to watch over her child and brother."

Medik cut in. "Sir, Sue is like me, working for Chronos to protect our family. I'll figure out a way to get you more on Chronos. Although it was hard enough to get Chameleon in as it is. The security is getting tight." Venkman nodded and thanked her again.

Supers: The White Light

Jeremiah lived on the streets, desperately searching through the trashcans hoping to score his next meal. He made so many bad choices in his life, he lost count. He'd been in and out of jail so many times, he began to miss it. In jail, he had three square meals a day, a roof over his head, access to books if he chose to read, work out… it seemed like paradise; better than where he was now. Out in the cold, starving, fighting for shelter each night, this was no way to live.

So when the whispers of a group of guys were planning a job with a big score spread to him, he accepted. What did he have to lose? If they got caught he'd just go back to the Pen and spend his next five to ten years in his "paradise."

The plan was set out, they were going to break into a warehouse and steal some unmarked crates for a buyer the lead guy knew. The score was going to be at least six figures for each of them and there were ten guys in total. Jeremiah had a plan in his mind too, if a few of these guys didn't make it through, the slice of the pie wouldn't have to be divided as much; a plan most of them shared, however.

At night, all dressed in black random clothes they were able to collect, the guys snuck onto the premises of the warehouse and with ease, took out the guards patrolling and use their access keys to get inside.

The warehouse was huge and filled with high-tech sophisticated equipment which none of these guys knew what for. Most of them didn't graduate high school or read a book, probably why they were here, to begin with.

But Jeremiah was curious and opened one of the crates. Inside it was a cryogenic machine with a subject in a cryostasis slumber. It startled him at first, but he moved towards the next crate marked with a biohazard sign. As he went to open it up, a grizzled voice echoed throughout the open area.

"You dumb punks are illegally trespassing; must be my lucky day." The dark mysterious figure was standing up by the skylight window, the moon's light beamed down from behind, casting a black silhouette to those on the ground.

Jeremiah might not have recognized this man, but the others sure did and knew his reputation. Everyone but Jeremiah scattered, hoping to flee from the wrath of the infamous Junker who, with both ball bats firmly in hand, dropped down.

Everything happened so fast, one bash to the skull here, one there, the lights flickered and Jeremiah remained behind the crates and just listened to the screams being silenced one at a time. Jeremiah's back pressed hard up against the crate marked; Bio-hazardous. He was startled when one of his colleagues bumped up behind him. After a small shriek alerted the Junker who then jumped around the corner.

Frightened, the one went running, but the Junker stepped in his way. "Where're you going princess, we're not done yet?" With a hefty swing of his bat, the fresh unconscious body soared high into the air and struck one of the halogen lights.

Jeremiah went to react, but the Junker was too fast and knocked him back and through the bio-hazardous crate. While lying in the pool of dangerous chemicals, the mist of the filament of the halogen bulb landed in the mix along with poor Jeremiah.

The tungsten and chemical (Which had been created from Ami Marik's blood) meshed as one and seeped into Jeremiahs skin. It got severely hot and began to burn poor Jeremiah from within. His body became so hot that the clothes on his burnt off and he emitted a bright flashing light, blinding the Junker.

The powerful light energy shot out in all directions, knocking the Junker way back, crashing through the wall and several hundred feet away. Seconds later the light dimmed and lying there unconscious was Jeremiah's body perfectly fine. To this day he has no recollection of what happened except for the white light that guided him to his new life; his second chance.

Now the White Light flies around the city at night, shining brightly. Proclaiming to be the beacon of light people can run to and feel safe. Even though he may be of African descent, he daunts a complete white attire, covering his entire body. His ski mask, white, his top hat, white, even his leather tailored-crafted trench coat, was completely white; I'd hate to be this guy's dry cleaner.

Over a short time, he's honed and mastered his abilities of light. He even willingly enlisted with the City's Heroes to fight crime. Like the Junker, he now had a cocky, overly confident attitude. He could turn himself into a being of pure light energy, expel that energy to blast or blind his opponents, and fly at the speed of… well you get the idea.

While aimlessly flying around the city, he searched for his next citizen to save. He and the Junker surprisingly got along, mostly because they share similar interests. They're both eager to beat up thugs and save the damsel in distress. Each night, before their shift, they would bet on who would save more people and how many thugs they'd hurt.

But for the past few days, he and the Junker have been working around the clock with all the craziness that's been happening. He crossed paths with a massive Super the other night and has been searching for some much-needed payback. The Super in question was a hulking Serpent beast, that roams around the skies, looking to devour others like it.

He was to call for back up since the first encounter he was almost consumed. He went in half-cocked, not thinking too hard, and was overwhelmed with how powerful the beast was. But once again last night, it had eaten another Super and that was on the White Lights conscious. So tonight he made a vow to slay this serpent of the night.

He and the Junker tried to track it earlier in the day, but it seemed impossible, for a massive serpent beast, it sure could hide. But at night, there it was, lurking around the skies, stalking its next potential prey.

But like last time, this night wasn't any different. The White Light flew in, blasted the Serpent, and distracted it long enough so the poor sucker who was about to be eaten could escape. But as powerful of a blast he could unleash was it didn't even seem to hurt the Serpent. It would retaliate and use its stinger tail and massive wings to try and swat and stab the Light, but they would harmlessly pass through. Their fights always ended in a stalemate, and that didn't sit well with the Light; he shouldn't have to ask for help.

It was now during the day and since the Serpent was in hiding, he was helping the Junker on the streets. He was making his usual flyby passes when the Tree made contact.

"Hey Light, the Junker found those bank robber Supers. They're hitting them in the good old consecutive order and not being random and unpredictable like most robbers; so they're at the Second National Bank."

"Roger that Woodman; be there in a flick of a light…"

Police had the building surrounded before the Junker even got there. Also on the scene were two SBU stiffs. But they didn't pose a threat to known Supers, especially those who worked for the city. They were more than cooperative when it came to disclosing information.

When the White Light landed, he was immediately approached by countless cheering fans, intriguing reporters, and of course, the SBU. After striking some poses, shaking some hands, and blowing kisses through his mask, he answered a few easy questions with, "I shine the light on crime," the infamous cheesy line he always ends press releases with.

It wasn't a secret that all-female SBU agents didn't like working with the Light or Junker for obvious reasons. They'd rather spend more time flirting and boasting rather than focusing on the problem at hand.

The female agent reluctantly disclosed information. "The big one inside seems to be invulnerable or at least immune to penetration…"

The Light couldn't help himself. "Like most of the SBU ladies I hear." Then he stuck out his chest and in a commanding tone, he shouted for all to hear. "But don't fear, I shall shed the light on these criminals and bring them to justice."

She muttered as she shook her head, "Oh brother." But the crowd cheered him on.

Both the Junker and Light stood in front of the bank where the front door used to be. It was obviously removed by someone with tremendous strength and hurled to the side. The police informed them that the bank was vacant except for the two who were robbing it. They don't fear the cops or SBU. The two robbers just took their time and eventually strutted out the front door when they were done cleaning it out.

The bulking seven-foot-tall muscular brute was the first to exit. In his hands, a few dozen bags of cash no Normal could carry. But it was quite obvious, this man wasn't a Normal.

He had an exciting grin when he saw two of the infamous heroes standing outside. He dropped the bags and began to clap and jump up and down like a kid in a candy store. "Oh joy, finally heroes for me to smash."

The Junker was the first to act, racing up with his lucky hockey stick in hand and swung. As the shaft struck the chest, the stick cracked in half. The Junker stood there puzzled.

With his massive fists, the brute backhanded the Junker, sent him flying backward and collided into the Light. The cops had no choice but to open fire. The dozens of bullets just harmlessly bounced off his impenetrable skin.

The big man chuckled as he stomped his way to the two Heroes slowly getting to their feet. He grabbed both men by the throats and lifted them. He slowly crushed their throats and they gasped for air, but couldn't contest their attacker's strength.

As he desperately tried to pry the fingers to free his throat, the Junker coughed up. "Ok Light, this one's yours."

The White Light closed his eyes and transformed into his pure transparent ethereal being and slipped through the brute's grip. He charged up both his hands together and unleashed a devastating blast. A direct hit his opponent's chest, knocking him back inside the bank and blinding all those staring by the extraordinary bright light emitted.

Shortly after, a well-built man stepped out from inside the bank holding only two bags of cash. Electricity surged around his body as he panned the outer scene. In the big crowd, he spotted the dozens of armed cops and the pair of SBU agents and Heroes. This man knew he was outnumbered, but not out powered.

"Is this all the sent? It won't be as electrifying," He spoke rather presumptuous. He dropped the bags to stick out his hands and when he did, powerful electrical rays shot out, frying the cops and SBU service weapons. The guns became too hot to hold as they ducked for cover behind their service cruisers.

As the Junker reached for another blunt weapon stuffed in his golf bag, he remarked. "I'll give this punk a lesson in bad puns." As he pulled out his ball bat and before charging in cried out, "Batters up!"

Before the Junker reached his target, the electric man smirked and fired a bolt of lightning straight at his chest. After landing hard next to the Light and staring down at his scorched sizzling shirt, the Junker remarked. "I guess you're up again Bulb boy."

Even though he wore a mask, you knew he was glaring at his comrade when he replied. "Are you sure you want me to steal all the glory here? Those two SBU agents you were trying to get with are here."

That line alone made the Junker shoot back up to his feet. "Let's tag team this punk."

The Light nodded and they started to move forward.

Sparkz, the robber in charge, just grinned. He stood there and allowed them to get a little closer. As the Junker entered striking distance, Sparkz turned back and hollered to his partner in crime. "Ok Negator, do your thing."

Both heroes stopped to look at each other, silently asking the other, "What's up?"

Shrugging it off as nothing, the Junker moved in to make his attack as the Light charged up. But right as they went to unleash their devastating blows something terrible happened to the two. Something every Super fears. Something the SBU scientists were able to create just over a year ago now. The Lights blinding energy fizzled into nothing, the Junker lost his strength and agility as he tripped over his own feet.

But it wasn't the serum that affected these two; it was something/one else instead. The big brute slowly stepped out from the shadows of the bank. The Negator was focusing his concentration on his rather unique ability. His hand was pointing at the two Supers' general direction.

Sparkz boasted as the two heroes felt completely useless without their gifts. "My big friend here isn't just incredibly strong and impenetrable but has this unique ability to prevent fellow Supers in a small area from using their powers. Don't worry, like those silly darts, it has a short effect. You'll be back to those ridiculous quips in no time."

After collecting the money bags and departing off, he nodded and said. "Now if you both don't mind, it's time to bolt." And with that said, he transformed into a bolt of electricity and shot off into the sky. His brute friend collected all his bags and took a powerful leap.

While still powerless, the two heroes just stood there as the cops and SBU agents encircled them, wanting answers. As the Captain started to yell, the agents cut in.

"I thought you two could handle anything?"

The Light felt the need to defend their failure, "Well if you SBU nerds did proper intelligence on these criminal Supers, you'd know what abilities they have. And then maybe us heroes wouldn't have to go in blind and find out the hard way."

"Yeah," the Junker stepped in and patted his comrade on the back. "Good job handing them back the blame. I didn't think of that."

Before the agents could rant and bicker back, Tree made contact via their ear radios.

"Light, Junk, we need you both back to HQ pronto. Venkman has returned and needs us here for an important meeting."

"Yeah, roger that Wood; umm, it might take us a little while to get there…" He left it at that and looked at the angry officer glaring by his cruiser. "Hey, do you mind giving my pal and me a lift home?"

SUPERS: MARIK

An emergency broadcast took over all the channels and the beautiful intrepid reporter explained the following. "This is footage from an anonymous source, of what truly happened just hours ago at the shelter built for young frightened Supers. What was once a peaceful place for scared little Supers, known to house a few dozen at a time, was viciously slaughtered and burnt to the ground. There were no survivors left in the smoldering ruins. But thankfully this unknown person sent in this clip because it reveals the sick twisted individuals who were responsible for this horrific travesty."

The clip showed the 2nd building where the Beginning called home. It showed Mallarian flying around the area, attacking and shooting his energy attack. Then it cut to Maverine near the ground floor with his big barrel canon, walking towards the building.

"It is still unknown who the one Super flying around is, but the notorious and most wanted Super, Maverine was there. Now, will the government pass that Super registration bill? Is this not a good enough reason to prove they are a danger to all of us? He is the twin brother of the City's Hero group leader, Venkman. So you can be assured, he won't do anything."

It was clear to both Pongo and Mal, who were watching the news from one of Pongo's undisclosed secret hideouts scattered throughout the Mega-City, that this was doctored footage. Little Brett was snuggled with his parents who were also watching, none of them could believe their eyes.

Pongo did his best to hide his smirk by reacting all frustrated and shaking his head. He turned the volume down so he could explain. "This is certainly Petersons work. Now, because of this, not only will we be hunted by the Chronos lackeys, but now the police and SBU. I just hope Venkman and the others are on our side now."

Mal tried to remember the event and asked. "But the SBU were there, they saw what happened… Didn't they?"

"Yeah they were, but as she said, this is the fuel the SBU needs to go forward with their plans." Pongo rubbed his chin. "This is a well put together video. Chronos certainly goes all the way when it comes to hiring the best. If I didn't know the truth, I would think this was real."

Mal was staring at the worried family and asked. "So what's our next move? We can't keep jumping from one safe house to the other. We have to get this kid and his family out of town."

"You're right, for one, this is my last safe house, and two, we can't leave town now. Not with the cops searching all traffic in and out and the SBU will be monitoring the skies. We need to lay low and find some way of letting Venkman or his guys of our whereabouts. The last place Chronos would think to look for us."

Mal had thought of one place he'd been to earlier that day. "There's a cabin in the woods we could go to."

Pongo was curious, after all, he knew of a place in the woods as well. But it had been presumably hit by Chronos and killed someone he was supposed to meet for information against Peterson. "Where in the woods is it?

"It's isolated from the rest, but still in spitting distance from the lake. It's on the Eastside, in the thick bush. It once belonged to…"

Slightly angered, Pongo finally realized the Super before him was the hitch in his plan. He finished the rest, "Wolfganger!"

Mal was taken back, confused that Pongo knew the name. "Yeah, that's it. How do you know him?"

Pongo was more concerned with how this man standing before him knew. "How about you go first, how do you know the Wolf?" He wasn't sure if he wanted an answer, considering the situation they were in together. But he discreetly reached into his pocket and pulled out his father's ring, just in case.

Mal noticed the action and immediately held out his hands, taking the defensive stance. He didn't want to fight this man; they were on the same side. He did his best to explain. "Hey, hold on there. I was sent by Kyle to retrieve two wolf specimens the man stole."

"He didn't steal them, those were his family. He had the ability to communicate and control wolves and other canines; among other wolf-like abilities. He found out what Peterson was making him do and the experiments he was conducting on the poor animals." But he calmed down and tucked the ring safely back into its resting place. After all, he knew Mal was being manipulated by his inside informant Kyle into doing things he didn't want to do.

Mal exhaled his nervous breath and went back to explaining his plan. "But I don't think they'd look for us at an old mission, it wouldn't make sense for us to go there."

Pongo smiled, he agreed. He also thought that if Maverine was out there as well, it would be one of the few places he'd venture to. And if so, he could make contact and since the footage was now out there, it would more than enough to convince him to help.

● ● ●

Ami Marik was incredibly beautiful with her long raven hair with bleach blonde streaks throughout. She was known to be one of the first Supers to announce to the world, her true self. Unlike most Supers, she did not take on a new alias; her super name. It was an unspoken rule with Supers to, once they discovered their powers, to grant themselves an alias. The reason why it started was to mask who they were, but now, it has become a pop trend; like a rite of passage. To most, it meant you have come to grips with the change and accepted who you truly are.

The court had called a recess to examine over all the topics and evidence brought forth before them on this "Supers registration" act. Not only did that mean anyone with special gifts had to immediately come forward or be sentenced to life on the island. It gave the government the excuse to equip all police officers the right to carry the serum on their person; like SBU agents.

Ami stressed and continually found herself repeating the same thing over and over again. This will only provoke the Super community and ruin what she's spent the past few years trying to accomplish.

But with the vast rising of criminal Supers, her plea was just being ignored. She brought up several key points to her argument. How the once known vigilante, now turned mercenary, Superbat was wrongfully imprisoned. One night on patrol, the SBU was able to track him down and then forced him to the island. He told her that all they did was stick him with needles and withdrew his blood.

It made one point prominent; why should any Super help those who don't seem to want it?

And the courts also brought up recent events. The one, in particular, was the Super attack on her own company, the Beginning. Why would she defend and argue for those who just assaulted her directly?

They then mentioned the juvenile Hero Group who just seemed to boast more than foil crimes. Clearly, they weren't up to snuff like the SBU. They gave Supers a chance, a chance they ultimately failed. So that wasn't helping her case either.

Knowing she was getting nowhere, Ami stormed out and headed for the washroom. After splashing some water on her face, her nerves deadened. She needed a different way in her argument to somehow win/ woo some votes in her favor. She was torn between the idea of using a certain someone's power of persuasion to achieve that goal. But like Venkman, she swore to never use her powers like that.

With little options and the clock winding down, she stood in the hallway in a moral conflict. Masking as security guards, two Agentman clones headed her way. They were sent here for one simple task, get many samples of her blood; one way or another. Cold and calculated the clones stormed right up to her, with one causing a distraction, the other would stick her.

The left guard had a coffee in hand and when he passed by, he eyed her blouse and "tripped", splashing the liquid all over. It seemed to work, after he apologized profusely, Ami just smiled and told him, "Not to worry, accidents happen."

But it wasn't an accident; purely intentional as the other guard came up behind her and injected the needle into Marik's neck. Her abilities were unknown to Peterson since after all, he hadn't spoken to her in months and with her ability, it was hard to stay up to date.

The syringe didn't have a chance to pierce her skin, instead, it snapped. Enraged, she backhanded the clone, knocking him back and across the hall into the wall. The one who spilled his coffee on her was baffled. He immediately jumped on the defensive to quickly avoid her onslaught of a powerful combination of punches and kicks.

During the fight, a half dozen SBU agents raced to the scene as Normals all around in a panic and fled the scene screaming. They found three potential Super threats fighting where combat was forbidden. The SBU saw their chance to apprehend one famous Super and two others. They tossed in a few smoke grenades that quickly unleashed that dangerous green gas.

The gas quickly surrounded all three causing them to all stop fighting and dropped to their needs coughing. The two guards soon vanished, leaving Ami Marik there alone. The SBU agents slowly inched forward with guns trained on her. She knew she couldn't resist and allowed them to bind her and prepared herself to take a trip to the Island.

●　●　●

It took about an hour for Pongo, Mal, and the Mitchells to walk through the forest and to the abandoned cabin in the woods. They took the scenic route, ensuring they were not being followed and to get a different perspective on Wolf's lodge.

The entire trip, the parents didn't say a word. Brett didn't speak either but was constantly reading the surface thoughts of those two strange men who came to his rescue. But he remembered what his dad told him a few months ago when all of this started happening to young Brett.

"Now son, just because you have all these special gifts, doesn't give you the right to pry into people's heads. In fact, I rather you didn't, in case the government can somehow track it. We need to keep you safe." His dad went on to explain the seriousness of the Super situation at that time and feared what might happen to Brett if anyone found out. So he made Brett promise not to use his abilities until he and his dad fully understood them.

But back at the house was different, they charged in and he could hear their thoughts as they approached the door.

"This will be an easy job Bat, snatch, and run."

"What about the family Bryan?"

"Kill them."

That didn't sit well with Brett, it only made him angry and when his rage took over, he had no control. He instilled his psychic fear into the mind of the Speedster and scared him off. As for the other, he used his telekinesis and flung him far, far away. Hoping neither would ever return.

But he's only a boy and doesn't know how persistent Peterson is. That man will send as many as needed to retrieve a gifted Super such as Brett.

Pongo whispered to Mal to hang back and watch the family as he went ahead to make sure it was in fact, vacant. If it wasn't, he didn't want the family at risk. Pongo cautiously approached the cabin, took each step one at a time, and peeked inside the opening.

Inside, searching through the disaster was a familiar face. This burly man in a trench coat, wearing those special high-tech goggles, brought an overwhelming joyous grin to Pongo's face.

He startled the lone man when he spoke. "Maverine, is that really you?"

It was he, the man he's been trying to reach for days now. Maverine turned around and saw who it was. "Hey Pongo, it's been a long time. What's going on around here, where is Tom?"

Pongo wasn't sure if he should tell him the truth, knowing how he would most likely react. Instead, he explained how Peterson was experimenting on his wolf buddies and Tom took them and escaped. Now he's on the run and hasn't spoken to him since.

Pongo signaled to Mal that it was safe and to bring the family in. As Mal entered, he saw Maverine standing there and immediately froze; he didn't know what to say.

Mav broke the ice, "Hey, it's Mal right?" Maverine then saw the family entered and seemed somewhat surprised to see them. "And who are they?"

Mallarian explained. "They're the reason why I can't go back to Chronos now. Peterson desperately wants this boy; he has abilities quite like your brother."

"I see," through his goggles, Maverine eyed the boy up and down. He rubbed his stubby chin and asked. "Ok, so what's our move here? We can't play keep away forever."

Pongo stepped in with his plan. "I think we need to get Brett out of town, but personally, I want to stop Peterson and when I say stop, I mean kill. He's done enough to all of us; I don't think anyone's going to argue the fact."

Maverine nodded, he too liked the idea. "And what about Venkman, are we going to get his group of Heroes together? We're going to need all the help we can gather."

Pongo, who knew Maverine for a long time was leery on the man's question and statement. He should have been more suspicious but under these circumstances, he ignored them and went along with it.

*   *   *

The Light and Junker returned to the HQ thanks to police escorts. When the elevator stopped on the main floor, standing there ready to go over the plan was both Venkman and Tree.

The second elevator arrived shortly after and when the doors opened, Miss Marik stumbled out. She appeared to be slightly wounded as she fell into the Junkers arms.

Venkman seemed to be the most concerned. "Ami, what happened?" He didn't like to unwillingly read the minds of people he considered friends unless he felt he had to. Most of them knew this, so they never asked about it.

"The courts, I was attacked. I think it was Peterson's main henchman, the Agentman."

The Junker carried her to the nearby couch in the meeting room. She was able to rest and collect herself before explaining more.

"The SBU charged in and tried to take me down. I didn't want to, but I knew if I went along, they'd just take me to their stupid Island. So I fought them off and…" She took a moment to pause, before finishing with, "I had no choice Venkman, I had to come here."

Venkman nodded and reassured her that she was always welcomed here, no matter what. "Now, you take some rest, the others, and I have an errand to run."

"Oh, what are you guys doing?" Both the Light Junker stepped in and asked the same question.

Venkman explained the events that have been happening, the boy who Peterson wants. And Kyle, the poor guy who's still trapped inside. He believes that Peterson should face justice and thinks Kyle might be the only person who is willingly able to give up his exact whereabouts.

The Junker also brought up the Beginning building and what he thinks happened. While in the back of the cruiser, he and the Light heard over the police radios. Was it true, or some hoax to draw out Maverine and this Mallarian fellow?

Venkman shook his head, "I can't see Maverine attack the building like that. It's got to be all Chronos, which means Pongo and Mal have the boy." He turned to the two who just recently lost their abilities and asked. "Are you two ready to get back out there?"

The Light flicked his fingers and emitted a blinding light. He tipped his hat and replied. "Time to hit the lights!"

The Junker punched his palm and in a stern tone replied. "Put me back in the game coach!"

SUPERS: KYLE

Kyle wasn't always the ladies' man, the smooth talker; that charming handsome individual who you'd turn on your mother to do what he asked. Before his change for the "better", Kyle was known, sorry, more like unknown to the world. He spent his childhood being ignored and usually the brunt of most jokes. The ladies wouldn't even give him the time of day. If he was about to be struck by a moving vehicle, nobody would notice or sadly even care.

Kyle had a droopy eye, crooked nose, a terrible speech impediment, always stuttering his words, and had chronic asthma. He was a severe case of one seriously ugly duckling turned into a beautiful swan you'd do anything for.

For his prom, he asked out the one girl who sometimes talked to him, not because she wanted to, but because no one really talked to her. When he finally found the courage and spat out the words asking if she'd go with him, she laughed in his face and said. "I rather go alone than with you."

He kept to himself as he went through community college. His folks didn't want to invest the money to send him to a better school. Which was unfortunate since he had a higher than average intelligence. They believed because he was so repulsive to anyone around him, he'd never be able to get ahead anywhere.

Kyle tried to exercise to gain some muscle, but couldn't even gain five pounds. He also took every beauty enhancer he could find, but nothing worked. But when that day he'd never forget came, Kyle woke up a completely changed man.

He went to the bathroom and saw a rather handsome stranger staring back at him. "What the heck, who are you?" His voice was deep and without his stutter. And when he did choose to speak, his brain would automatically make it so he sounded highly sophisticated and savvy.

His physical appearance drastically changed and for the better. He gained that muscle he wanted, his hair fully grew in, his nose and eye were, for lack of a better word, perfect. He was now the prime specimen of the word. Yes if you were to put a picture in the dictionary to visually describe the word, there was no one else's face that would fit. He didn't know why, but he wasn't going to complain.

So he got dressed and sauntered through the hallways like a man on a mission. Everyone, not just the girls, stopped dead in their tracks to get a full look at this mystery man. The girls wanted to be with him, the guys wished they looked like him. Kyle would wink and fire off his finger cannon at them all. Normally, the finger gun would get a, who is this guy, response. But when he did it, everyone started doing it back.

He approached his classroom and made his way in. The once loud room was silenced as they all fixated their jaw-dropping gaze and watched as he sat where the kid no one ever talked normally did.

The perplexed teacher eventually asked. "Umm, who are you?"

When Kyle disclosed his full name, it just surprised everyone. He then apologized for his tardiness and the teacher, who always gave him a hard time because of it, waved it off. "It's ok; we'll start whenever you are ready."

Confused, Kyle sat there, trying to figure out if this was a ruse or not. With everyone staring right at him, he replied. "I'm ready now, please start."

"Will do," The teacher said and started to conduct the lesson of the day.

Kyle was too distracted to pay any attention to the lesson. Between him figuring out what happened, the constant staring/gawking at him was overwhelming. He was never used to so much attention, he was used to having none. And every few seconds, a girl would sneak a peek back towards him, smile, and wave. When he waved back, they giggled and handed him their phone number.

When one of the girlfriends of a big scary jock handed him her number, the boyfriend jumped up. He grabbed Kyle from behind and prepared to give him a brutal beating. But when he spun Kyle around to face the man, Kyle pleaded.

"Please, you don't want to hit me, Jack."

Jack's fist lowered and in a calm stated, he replied. "You're right; I don't want to hit you. I'm sorry, my bad."

Ok, Kyle was beside himself now. How did he just talk his way out of a fist from an enraged boyfriend?

Over the years, Kyle figured out that not only did he have his Super looks, he also had Super charm. All he had to do what ask for something, whether it was a job promotion, asking a girl home, getting someone to do something, they did it. He could walk into a bank, ask the tellers for money and without batting an eye or questioning him, they'd just hand it over.

Kyle wasn't always the most honest person, for the first few years with his powers; he leaned towards the criminal angle. He would backstab and provoke others to turn on one another. It wasn't until he met her, his love, that he changed his ways. He's never, to this day, used his charm on her. She was the only person to fall for him naturally.

They got married and had children, Kyle had dropped the charm act altogether. He swore to her he'd never use it for personal gain ever again. Until that day he came home to find they had been abducted by Peterson.

At the time, SBU Agent Pongo came to Kyle, in their day, when Kyle was a criminal, he had him arrested. But now, when Kyle told him he'd changed, Pongo believed him. Pongo reminded him about that favor he swore to repay and if Kyle agreed, he'd take him off the SBU radar. The mission was simple, infiltrate Chronos and figure out what Peterson is up to. Kyle was a man of his word and honored it.

But he was compromised, somehow Peterson knew he was a spy and kidnapped his family. A furious Kyle stormed into Peterson's office, told the two Agentman clones to take a walk, and was now alone with the CEO of Chronos. Kyle swore all he wanted was his family returned safely and he'd tell Pongo he couldn't find anything.

But Peterson didn't care about Pongo; he needed Kyle for his own reasons...

This is how he wound up here, trapped in his cell on level four of the Chronos building. He wasn't alone, there were the collection of Supers he helped abduct. None were bound because the entire floor was engulfed in a faint green negate gas. It was what was preventing Kyle from charming his way out.

So he sat on the cold metal cot and just started thinking and feeling sorry about the things he was forced to do over the past few weeks. If these Supers trapped along with him only knew the truth, his charm might not save him. He just hoped that Mallarian was able to beat the others to Brett and keep him away from Peterson.

The fate these Supers endure wasn't something for an innocent young boy to experience. Kyle accepted his fate; he just wished his family didn't have to suffer for his choices.

The wall on the opposite side of the prison room came crashing down by one powerful blast. Floating in through the fresh gaping hole was a beacon of light that represented those imprisoned inside, freedom. The White Light continued in and once inside, he found himself exposed to the gas and quickly lost his abilities.

When the elevator doors opened, out stormed a small group of armed security with orders to shoot any intruders on sight. And that they did. Wasting no time, their guns already drawn, they opened fire on the prone, defenseless beacon of light.

The bullets ripped through the air and just as they were about to strike Light in the chest, they just bounced off of the translucent telekinetic field surrounding him. Hovering behind the Light, just on the outer section of the wall, was Venkman. With a pushing motion, he sent a telekinetic wave of force, knocking all the guards over. He then pressed on his temple and took over the mind of one guard.

In a zombie state, that guard stood up, pulled out his keys, and opened Kyle's cell.

The Light in his normal state scanned for the source of the gas but found no controls. Venkman motioned for Kyle to take his hand before back up arrived.

Venkman wanted to take all the caged Supers along, he couldn't just leave them there, knowing what was in store for them. But there just wasn't time; he'd have to come back.

The Light found the vents, but no shut-off switch anywhere. He panned down the wall and saw numerous vents, each pumping the gas into every cell. The machine pumping it must be on another level, perhaps the basement. He informed the others.

Venkman stressed his concern just as the Junker contacted him via their ear radios and informed him that he just busted down the office on the upper floor and it was empty; no Peterson or his lackey henchman present. The place had been wiped out. Nothing but cheap old office supplies and furniture was left. The Junker had searched every floor, all of them except for the fourth were empty.

Venkman had used his telekinesis to help both Kyle and the Light fly harmlessly out the blown hole and across the street to the adjacent building's roof. Not too long after, they met up with the Junker and together, headed back to the Heroes base to regroup and figure out what to do next.

SUPERS: BRYAN

It wasn't a secret that Bryan and Sue were siblings, but not many knew they were fraternal twins. This probably explains why their abilities are similar, but not completely the same. Bryan can move incredibly fast, surpassing the speed of sound with ease. Sue has the ability to teleport, reaching a few kilometers away at the blink of an eye. Both possess the ability to mold their hands into simple melee weapons. While Sue usually turns her fingers into razor-sharp blades, Bryan likes making his fist larger and as hard as steel. Both are also tough, strong, and extraordinary agile.

And both couldn't be any different, Bryan's always been the hothead; edgy can't stay in one spot kind of guy while Sue is more the calm, good-hearted kind of girl. So it wasn't a surprise that they ended up on totally separate sides of the law.

But now, both working for Chronos; Bryan has proven his loyalty time and time again, which is why he speaks to Peterson personally and knows of his diabolical plan. He doesn't care, he has no morals, it all went into his sister. He cares about family and money, not necessarily in that order either. He made a deal too if he agrees to help, not only will he be greatly rewarded, also his blood will never be harvested for powers along with his sister and nephew.

Sue's kid, Bryan's nephew is little Billy "The Kid"; who's only ten years old and one malicious sinister child with an extreme ego problem. He has made it clear to not only his mom and uncle but others inside

Chronos that he will be one of the most feared Supers out there. No one except for Sue knows the true identity of the boy's father; not even Billy knows who. Why is Sue keeping it a secret is known to only her; maybe to protect the father's identity, make sure his enemies don't come looking for an edge. Perhaps even he doesn't know. Maybe she hopes by Billy not knowing, he won't want to follow in his footsteps, or fears he already has...

● ● ●

Bryan stood with his hands trembling behind him, waiting for Peterson to spin around in his black leather chair and let him know why he's been summoned. The trembling wasn't a sign of fear, it was just fidgeting. Bryan didn't like to be still; he had to be moving. Patience wasn't his strong virtue, but Peterson thrived on it. As he slowly chopped the end of his cigar off, he finally addressed the jittery man.

"Mister Bryan, we have a serious problem. First, we lose the super being data, then the child, and with Agentman's little slip up at the courts, Miss Marik is now being detained at SBU Island. They say it's practically impenetrable. What do you say?"

"I say a man with his skills should be able to get a few of his people inside." Bryan was a hothead, and this slow-paced conversation bored him. "Sir, I'm not the espionage guy here, you have and had plenty. Your face-changing lapdog, my sister's really good at those kinds of things, and heck, even Billy would be better suited. And that Chameleon you let slip away awhile back, all better for this sort of gig."

Peterson nodded as he lit his cigar and explained. "I don't disagree with you; you're right, you are the last person who should be doing a mission like this. But Agentman's preoccupied with his special assignments, the Kid is too new to the game for a mission like this. This requires a delicate touch and a set of skills that I feel he doesn't possess at his age; but I'm certain over time, he will. And your sister..." He paused, to inhale the toxic fumes from his hand-rolled Cuban and continued. "I'm questioning loyalties as of recent, for obvious reasons of course. So I would like you to handle this matter, get it done hopefully before she steps one foot onto the boat."

Bryan didn't care about the primary mission given, he was more concerned about the one promised to him when he first came to Chronos. The reason he rarely spoke to his sister for almost a year until she resurfaced and joined the company. "Sir, what about Maverine? You told me I was going to be the one who got to kill him. But I hear you got someone else to handle that. We had a deal, no harm to Sue and the Kid, and I got to be the one to kill Maverine."

"Relax Mister Bryan; Agentman didn't have a chance to succeed. But remember I told you, you must have patience. He'll come into your sights and when he does, he's all yours. But I still need him alive for the moment."

Bryan wasn't impressed, grinding his teeth with frustration; he knew his day would have to wait. He was a professional and did the job asked. "You know to relax and patience aren't in my job description right?" Before he bolted off, he bowed as he did after every meeting.

●　●　●

Sue found herself twenty or so stories high above the city. She was on the Heroes platform. She stood there in the strong winds waiting to speak with the man who requested to see her.

It wasn't long for the others to return. Once everyone landed on the platform, the others brought Kyle inside, leaving Venkman and Sue alone. After giving each other a heart-filled hug and Venkman thanking her for coming, he explained.

"I'm not sure how up to speed you are on the events of today…" He paused, allowing her to cut in, or confirm that she was or not. She just nodded and allowed him to go on. "Good, well, as you know then, Pongo has been investigating Chronos for some time now. And asked for our help, but you know we couldn't because of diplomatic reasons. That's why I asked your ex to join Chronos, to begin with…"

With a playful smile, she cut, " I think you mean, your brother."

It wasn't a secret that Maverine had a bad reputation. But neither was the fact that he was Venkman's twin brother or Sue's ex-love interest. Maverine was constantly running around the globe, handling secret government jobs and then having to answer for any botched missions or ones he handled with unjust reasons. So nobody wanted to admit they knew him. Doing so usually placed you in a small white room inside SBU headquarters answering the same old questions. "Where is Maverine and when is the last time you communicated with him?"

It was a running gag between all his friends to admit what role in his life they played and denied their own.

He remarked with a grin. "I have been mistaken for that in the past." He turned serious and asked. "I need you to do your thing and locate Pongo and Mal. I'm going to need them to help us with Chronos and figured you could be the sitter for this child. Maybe take him and the family someplace warm, like in the Southern hemisphere, or even the other side of the world. But don't say where, leave it at your discretion."

Sue nodded and requested one thing in return. "Just promise me you'll keep my boys safe."

"Don't worry, I'll watch all three." With a slight curl of her lip, she shook her head and before Venkman's very eyes, she vanished.

● ● ●

Billy "The Kid" and the Bat were in the last abandoned safe house that belonged to Former Agent Pongo. The Kid let loose a long-drawn-out sigh, signaling he was bored. He kicked over an empty can and pouted. This was the fifth supposedly known location that Pongo owned and like the first four, nobody was home.

"This blows Bat man; I'm not the investigating type. I wanna shoot something; it's why I have a kick-ass energy blast. This is old people's work."

Superbat, who was in his human form so he didn't attract or scare the Normals, didn't like this part of the job either. But he wasn't going to be a whiney child about it. "We're short on staff; someone needs to do the recon work. If you want to play with the grownups, then you have to start doing the grownup work."

"You're lucky there's no money for killing you; well, there's always glory." The Kid glared, just because he was ten, he hated being treated like a child. He's proven that he's just as dangerous as the big gamers, but wondered how many hoops he was going to have to jump through to prove it and get some respect.

Superbat chuckled and replied. "Listen junior, when this is all done, I say we hit the danger room and see who's more bad-ass. And after I whoop your little behind, you damn well better treat me with some respect."

Nothing enraged the Kid more than hearing, boy, junior, or son. Not even his own mother calls him by that. He pushed the heated argument further. "Please, I'd blast you before you went all batty."

Superbat didn't respond, it would only escalate the situation, and right now, was about the job at hand; plus, someone had to be the adult in this partnership.

• • •

Sue teleported all around town visiting all the plausible Pongo locations she could recall. She came across her son and Superbat, who were turning the place inside out. She stuck to the shadows when she saw a third member of the Chronos team entered the room. It was Agentman, a rare treat to see him. He was usually busy standing behind Peterson and ensuring his safety. So why was he out and about?

He was talking to the other two, but Sue could hear everything.

"My sources have to find the child. He's with the traitor and former SBU agent at the cabin in the woods."

The Kid let out a wicked grin as he rubbed his hands together and excitedly asked. "Awesome, we'll get some payback for that earlier stunt of theirs. Are we gathering everyone?"

Agentman shook his head. "No need. Your uncle has an assignment and as for your mother, Peterson questions her loyalty, and who's she's truly working for."

Billy glared and remarked. "Yeah, she's a real bummer. Don't worry, when we get back, I'll take care of her."

Superbat wasn't a ruthless mercenary. He was here because it beat where he was. Even he was uneasy with what the Kid said. However, Agentman shared the same cold-hearted attitude and nodded.

Sue had everything she needed; the whereabouts of the child in question and Peterson's intentions of what to do about her when this was all said and done. She knew she'd have to get there first. He most likely has his small army of clones on their way to retrieve the package and leave no survivors. She just hoped that he didn't already have a clone on the inside...

SUPERS: BRETT

Pongo stood by the fire as he watched Mav with a questionable demeanor. Something wasn't right with the man. It was what he said when they first met up, "We're going to need all the help we can gather." That's not something the maverick, the man who hates working in groups, would ever say or admit to even if it were true. Plus, there were little minor details he's picked up on over this past hour being cooped up inside this cabin.

Tips like the following: Maverine has known Tom "The Wolf" for many years, decades even, and usually referred to as his other brother. If that were so, then why didn't he step out to the grave and pay his respects? Where was his infamous bag of heavy artillery he was known to always have with him? But the last thing he saw was the real kicker, he watched as Maverine remove his protective goggles to rub his eyes. His eyes are so sensitive to the light, that the crackling fire would be too bright for him to take them off and not squirm. Plus, his eyes had a subtle glow to them, this person, who Pongo was now convinced wasn't Mav, didn't.

Pongo went to confront this mystery person for answers but caught out of the corner of his eye, little Brett and his family. If whoever this was reacted with hostile actions, they might get caught in the crossfire; he couldn't risk that. So he hung back and kept a cautious eye on the Mav impersonator.

Maverine broke the silence. "We need a better plan this sitting tight. Chronos will eventually find us."

Mal replied. "Yeah, but what can we do? Everyone is looking for us."

Mav agreed. "You're right, they are looking for us." He went on to explain his idea. "But I think someone should play decoy, lead the SBU one way, while the other with the kid, go the another."

Mallarian gave the sacrificial lamb idea some serious thought. He had no reason to doubt or distrust the man standing across from him. This was the reputable Maverine giving his advice. The man's been around longer than these people have been alive, he has wisdom over them all. Plus he knew arguing or making him angry didn't go over well for the recipient. So the two of them went over the plan to get the psychic kid and his family out of town.

Meanwhile Pongo stepped into the other room to join Brett and the family. He stared at the child who was in his mother's arms, doing his best to keep her from crying. Without saying a word out loud, he knew the kid could read minds and hopefully was keeping an "ear out" so to speak. In his mind, he tried to communicate with Brett via psychokinetic waves and said. *"Hey Brett, can you hear me? Don't say anything out loud, just look at me and nod."*

He waited to see if Brett would comply but he didn't. After all, he was obeying his father's wishes and being considerate of others' privacy. He tried multiple times before realizing the kid wasn't listening.

Pongo came back to check on the imposter just in time to hear them fine tweak the details. The plan was only a problem if Mal knew the truth as he did. Sure, if this was the real Maverine, who was willing to babysit a psychic child and his family, then he'd be the perfect person for the job. But that's the thing, he wouldn't even offer, it wasn't what he was made to do. He'd be better suited to causing the distraction and providing suppression fire to allow the others to escape. These were just the fine-tuning details Pongo needed to ensure this wasn't the real Maverine.

"I'm not sure the world's most notorious man should be the one to escort the family out of town." Pongo stepped between the burly man and a confused Mal as he continued. As he talked, he slipped his hand into his pocket, wiggled his fingers around, fishing for the ring. "I agree though, but I think Venkman and the Heroes should hide the family while we distract the SBU."

Pongo managed to find the ring and pull it out. But his hand slipped and dropped the ring. «But we need to be careful, Chronos has spies,» He stared directly at Maverine and finished with, «Literally everywhere.»

Mal felt the tension but didn't know why. He didn't know either man well enough to pick up on their subtle hints. But Maverine or the person claiming to be him knew exactly what Pongo was accusing him of. He stared back, both trying to force the other to back down.

Mal tried to break them apart. "Whoa, guys, what's going on here? Maverine is the best choice for this job, isn't he? I mean, his reputation says enough."

With his eyes fixated on the man before him, Pongo replied. "You're right Mal, Maverine would be the best choice. But there's just one problem..."

Completely confused, Mal asked. "What's that?"

Maverine turned to face the baffled man to explain. "It's because I'm..." His face quickly changed right before their very eyes. The man once posing as Mav was now replicating Pongo. "Not who you think I am." With a wicked grin, the clone got the surprise on Mal kicked him in the chest. Mal fell to the ground, landing a few feet away.

Agentman moved with great speed. He was able to grab Pongo by the collar before he was able to draw his weapon. After two vicious head butts, Agentman spun him around and tossed him into Mal as he got back to his feet.

Meanwhile outside, eight clones armed with machine guns circled the cabin and were slowly closing in. Moments later, they were joined by Superbat flying in with the Kid on his back.

The fake Pongo calmly walked into the room with the frightened family. As he was in mid-change as he coldly stared down poor Brett and warned him. "Don't try any of your psychic crap or we will execute one of your parents. Do you understand?"

Brett was speechless as the tears rolled down his cheek. But he did nod to comply.

As Agentman reached for the boy, Sue suddenly appeared between them. After a backflip kick, she ported behind him, grabbed his collar, and tossed him out of the room.

In the split moment she had, she knelt beside the boy. "I'm Sue, I'm here to get you out. You need to trust me."

He quickly read her mind and saw that she was truthful and a legitimate person. He nodded. "Please, protect us."

Sue knew she could only take two for the ride; which meant someone was going to have to stay behind. Somehow, by her look, the dad knew and he gave her the nod that a father in this situation would; protect my wife and child.

The father took a moment to hug his family, silently saying goodbye. He gave Sue the go-ahead nod and took the wife in a child into her arms.

Seeping in like a ghost through the wall, was Billy "the Kid" Sue's son, who stepped into the room. Billy glared as his hands charged for a full blast. "You traitor!" He cried out to his mother.

The tears pooled around Sue's eyes. Her son was lost to her. Just as Billy unleashed his devastating blast, Sue, the wife, and the psychic child vanished. The surge of powerful energy zipped past and struck the innocent father instead.

Just as Mal and Pongo got back to their feet, the clones unleashed the swarm of bullets onto the cabin. Both men dropped back to the ground barely dodging the bullets. With the bullets cutting down the logged walls, it was only a matter of seconds before it collapsed.

Mal had to yell to be heard over the bullet onslaught. "I guess this means they got Brett."

Crawling along the floor, desperately searching for his father's ring Pongo shouted back. "I don't think they'd be shooting otherwise."

"That's not good, what's our next move?"

Just as Pongo recovered his ring, the bullets stopped. He slipped it on, activated the shield as Superbat swooped in through the gaping hole. The Kid joined in from the other room too. The Agentman clones unsheathed their swords and began to enter.

Collectively, Mal and Pongo blasted the Bat in the chest. The attack barely left a char mark.

Pongo shouted. "We'll have to figure that out later, need to regroup." He then took to the air.

Mal went to follow but the Kid was quick and blasted him in the chest, knocking him straight through the cabin wall.

Pongo came to a halt, to check up on his partner. With his guard down, the Bat leaped up and tackled him down to the ground. After several fierce blows, the force field dispersed and the last hit knocked the former agent right out.

The Kid rushed to the room where he sent Mal only to find it vacant. Billy turned to the skies and saw a small spot that was once Mal.

The Agentman clones found both the Bat and Kid arguing over Pongo's unconscious body, on who got to kill him. But Agentman knew, Peterson would rather have him alive to answer questions.

"Nobody's killing him, yet. We will take him to Mister Peterson first."

Off in the distance, Mallarian did a fly-by, searching for Pongo. Using his super vision, he examined the cabin. He spotted the Bat carrying poor Pongo. There was no sign of Brett or his family. Something just wasn't right. But now wasn't the time to go ask those questions. Mal knew he was severely outnumbered and needed help. He only had one place to turn to for that help and made his way there.

SUPERS: MALLARIAN PART 3

With Pongo kidnapped, Brett and his family missing, a lone Mallarian had no choice but to return to the Heroes headquarters and beg for their aid. As he landed, the doors slid open, and out came Venkman with his band of heroes. The whole party was there; infamous Junker, White Light, Tree, Marik, Kyle, and the Chameleon, all standing behind their leader.

Venkman greeted him like he knew he was coming. "Welcome back Mallarian. I presume Pongo and Sue were able to get the child out of town?"

Mal knew only of one Sue; the one working for Chronos. He had doubts that she was one Venkman was referring to. But still, there was something about her that didn't fit. She, out of all the members, did treat him kindly. Maybe she was one of the good guys, and like Kyle, forced to work for the company. If Venkman namedropped her, he must have trusted her, and maybe he should too.

Mal then put one and one together; she was a teleporter and could have popped in, took the boy and his family, and pop back out. It explained why they opened fire on the cabin. And why they took Pongo alive. But still, he wasn't certain and didn't want to give false hopes.

So Mal shrugged and did his best to explain. "Um, I'm afraid I don't know. You see we met up with Mav at this cabin in the woods..."

Venkman stepped back and questioned the statement. "You must be mistaken; Mav is in the med-bay, recovering as we speak."

Mal clarified what he meant. "Sorry, it wasn't the real one. But we didn't figure that out until it was too late. They also got Pongo. It was one of Peterson's guys disguising himself as Mav..."

Kyle piped up. "It was Agentman."

Mal seemed happy to see Kyle out and alive and expressed his gratitude for his help. But Kyle only nodded and kept quiet. Time was short and Venkman had a plan.

Venkman explained the situation. "Chameleon here was able to locate the other Chronos facilities. But he is uncertain as to which one hosts Peterson and the kidnapped families. And now perhaps Pongo. I think we should conduct a simultaneous strike on both, that way he can't slip past us."

Everyone standing behind Venkman seemed onboard with this plan.

With no other option or plan of his own, Mal agreed and asked. "Sounds good to me. So where are these buildings?"

Venkman stepped to the side and motioned towards the man in the tight green suit designed to resemble what a chameleon might look like if it was mutated with a human. The Chameleon had a black leather utility belt, with a shoulder strap with several pouches along his chest. He pulled out his handheld computer and opened the 3D graphic display.

"This is the image of the structure of the underground facility. As you can see, it's going to be almost impossible to just walk in." Chameleon explained.

Venkman stepped in. "That team, which will be Mal, Junker, and Cham, will have to somehow sneak in."

He allowed the sleuth to continue.

Chameleon switched images to another location. "And this is the air fortress. That's right, if you look up you'll see that some of the clouds don't quite match the others; that's the floating Chronos building. I'm kind of surprised no one's noticed it to be honest."

Venkman took over speaking once again. "And that's where Light and I will be striking."

The three left out stared at one another real quick before jumping in. Tree was the first to bring it up. "Sir, you forgot about the three of us."

Venkman replied he knew the kind of man this strong-rooted man was, but also that he wasn't much of a soldier. "I know old friend. But someone needs to hang back and coordinate both groups. Not to mention, someone needs to watch over Maverine."

Dragging his duffle bag full of weapons, and without his protective goggles, Mav beckoned from inside, overhearing the conversation. "Don't count me out on this. I'm itching for some payback."

He let the bag go to hold his ribs. His left leg dragged behind him. It wasn't a secret that his abilities still hadn't been restored. But even without his powers, Maverine was a veteran soldier. His combat skills were more than most of these heroes combined. He was proficient with weapons, master strategist, infiltration and extraction were just too great to ignore.

When asked about the missing eyewear, Mav and Tree came to the same conclusion; since his powers were negated, maybe his sensitivity went with it.

But he was still weak and that's what concerned everyone the most. Yeah, he was the lone rogue, the feared one, but he still had loyal friends. Even if sometimes he didn't admit to it.

Venkman was the only one willing to say no to the man. "Come on, you can't even lift your bag and you're vulnerable." He turned to the other two and explained why he didn't want them coming out. "As for the two of you, Peterson's looking for the both of you, presumably for his crazy scheme. So if you're the key to it, I want you as far away from him as possible."

But Kyle stepped in. "I want to help. I'll accompany them to the underground base."

Venkman nodded but stressed no to the other two. "Fine, but until we know what's really going on, Ami will remain here with Tree and Mav." He used his telepathy to tell Maverine there is no one else strong enough to protect her if Peterson is to send his goons.

Maverine couldn't argue the facts.

The Junker weighed in his thoughts with a chuckle. "So what, is it still his diabolical scheme to give normal dweebs special powers? It doesn't sound so bad to yours truly, heck, I almost did it the first time."

Tree explained the seriousness to him. "Well, it doesn't work on everyone; you need to have a certain blood type. And he's not doing it for Normals' sakes. I presume, like any good scientist, he's only using them to ensure the procedure worked. Even after the success with Chameleon, Peterson was hesitant."

Mallarian spoke next. "I was a success too."

Tree seemed relatively surprised, took a minute to examine the evidence, and came to a conclusion. He shared it. "Ok, so he and Wells have figured it out. So they're rounding up Supers for..." He looked at Kyle, who didn't share any information. Tree took it as a sign he was right and continued. "Something I don't know, however. But then they go attack the Beginning, why, we're still uncertain. Maybe Kyle can shed some light on it."

Kyle just shook his head and said he didn't know Peterson's plans, just only what he was willing to share, which wasn't much.

Maverine made his speculation. "Well, Peterson's been itching to perfect that super being serum, now he's gathering fellow Supers. And these two are successes. I'm no nerd in a lab coat, even I see the connection. He needs them and their powers to give it to himself. How? I leave that to the Wells'."

Mal asked. "So we've been collecting others to experiment on this whole time?" Mallarian was enraged and went to confront Kyle. "You tricked me, why would you…"

Maverine stepped between them. "Your fight isn't with him; he's in the same boat as us, ok."

The Light shared his story. "I'm confused here, dudes. So this Peterson guy wants to steal other Supers powers for himself. And has figured out a way to do it? And the government and SBU aren't doing squat about it? Typical."

Venkman cut in. "It doesn't matter how or what Peterson is up to now. All we need to know is that he's gone too far. Yes, the government isn't going to like what we're about to do, but it needs to get done. I don't want to ask you all…"

Maverine interrupted. "Save your morality speech for a group who cares Venkman. We're all in. Let's get to it."

The Junker coordinated with his team; Kyle, Mal, and Chameleon, and came up with a plan on how they were going to approach the underground facility. Kyle was able to inform them of an access passage through the sewers and should try that way first.

Meanwhile, Venkman addressed Mav, Marik, and Tree with their involvement in all this. He said that the three of them were the backup.

When the confirmation shows them where the families are being held, they are to head there and provide support.

Maverine didn't like being the backup, he was the frontlines kind of man. But given his current state, he had no other choice. He went to say something but Ami assured him that he'll get his chance to cause some damage and that calmed him down enough.

Both groups headed their way to the separate bases, hoping to put an end to this terrible day before it gets even worse.

Venkman turned to the Light and remarked. "We're going to be outnumbered when we get there. Any suggestions?"

The Light had just one. He saw the sun was setting and said. "Let me go get a friend."

Impatiently waiting for the call, Tree made his way to his lab to occupy his mind while Mav stood by the landing platform, staring out the window. Marik stood a few feet behind him, grinning wickedly like she was expecting something to happen.

"Too bad we didn't get a chance to finish the job," Ami said out of the blue as she bent down and unzipped his infamous bag. "We've always wanted to see what you stash inside here."

Maverine was confused as he spun around to see what she was going on about. Once he saw her rifling through his weapons, he knew this wasn't who she claimed to be. But he was without his powers, so he had to play this smart. "I like to hang on to my favorites; every gun in there tells a story."

She found a colt 45 pistol and carefully admired it. "What's the story of this weapon? Was this used to kill anything of significance?"

Mav inched closer; he knew where she was going with it. After all, that was the same gun he used to kill one of the clones belonging to Agentman; but that was long ago. He now was certain; this was one of those clones.

With a smirk, he wanted to provoke the clone into doing something brash. "Not really, the Super I had to gun down was petty. That particular story isn't glamorous, it was no real challenge."

"No real challenge huh, that's why your big brother had to come in and save the day." It wasn't Marik any longer, as he transformed to mirror his opponent and brought the pistol around to shoot. But Mav was already prepared and dove, tackling the imposter. Both struggled for the gun but since Mav was now a Normal, his strength was gone so he had to resort to other means.

After several blows to the face of Agentman, Mav was able to knock the gun from his hand. With the gun, just a few feet from them, both struggled with one another as Tree barged in to see what the noise was all about. Surprised to see two Maverine's fighting, he raced over and with his massive strength, pried the two from one another and held them with one hand each.

The hulking humanoid tree demanded answers. "What is going on in here? And which one of you is the real one? And where is Miss Marik?"

The real Mav went to declare it was he, but the clone spoke first. But it didn't convince the Tree; in fact, he turned to the real one and examined him more closely. "I've known you for a long time and would like to think I'd recognize the real you no matter what…" He turned to the one on his left and went on. "But this baffles me, to the fake one, superb job indeed."

The real Maverine wasn't impressed, after all, he could tell the difference. "Seriously Woody, you can't tell the difference?"

That was what Tree was looking for, a name he's asked Maverine and Junker multiple times in the past to not call him by; he hated that name. After he let the real one go, Tree glared at the one in his left hand and demanded answers. "Ok, where are the hostages and your boss?"

The clone knew he couldn't match Tree's mighty strength, but no matter what, he wasn't going to give him want he sought after either. It was then however that he sensed the presence of his duplicate companions slowly closing the gap and just let out a giant smile. "I'd duck if I were you."

With that said he disappeared as he was called back by the original just as the five Agentman clones, kicked the door in and rushed in with guns out ready to unleash a swarm of hot lead. Tree pulled Mav in and shielded him from the herd of bullets, taking them all into his bark-like skin. With their guns empty, Tree fell to the side, leaving Maverine alone to deal with multiple foes.

With his bag not too far away and the clones busy reloading, an enraged Mav took the opportunity and dove for it. As he landed, he reached inside, pulled out two sub-machine guns conveniently already loaded, and unleashed hell. The clones ducked behind the wall as two of them took the hits and fell over backward to the ground.

With his weapons empty, he picked up his pump-action shotgun and marched for the hiding cowards. He didn't care if he was without his abilities, they just murdered a friend and he was going to seek revenge.

As the clones finished reloading, they peeked around the corner just as Maverine got there; who in return, used the butt end of the shotgun and smacked two of them in the face, busting their noses. With the adrenaline pumping through him, Mav shot down another just as he took a bullet to the chest. But instead of piercing his skin, he regained his abilities and the bullet bounced off, leaving a small welt.

When he realized his powers were back, the clones did as well, and feared filled their eyes; they knew even with their numbers, they stood no match against a Super Maverine. With the one left standing, the others on the ground, Mav grabbed him by the throat and stated. "Which base is Peterson located? No fooling around now, you shouldn't have pissed me off."

The clone struggled to breathe, but he wasn't going to do it; not even if he was staring death in the face. Instead, he let loose a bloody grin as the clones on the ground, one by one, began to disappear. Maverine had been in several altercations with this Super before and knew he could only recollect his duplicates if he was within range, which meant the one in his hand, must be the original. Finally, after all this time, he had Agentman where he wanted. He wasn't going to show restrain here, this being was responsible for many deaths; one of him lying on the floor in the other room.

But he knew if he crossed this line, killing an unarmed person, he'd never be forgiven, just as he and his brother finally started talking once again. But then again, that's what made Maverine the one who was most feared, he didn't second guess, he went with what was right. He and his brother could mend fences another day, this Super had to be dealt with.

As he went to make the final squeeze, he vanished from his grasp. "Damn, another clone." Out of the corner of his eye, to the left, he saw swift movement and brought his shotgun around to take it out. Standing there with a cocky wave was the original Agentman who then smashed the giant window behind him and leaped out.

Racing over to get a shot or two off, Mav got to the ledge but was out of range as he saw the Super open a parachute and safely descended to the ground. Knowing there'd be another day, Mav ran back to his wooden friend and attended to his needs.

Tree was lying there coughing up sap, meaning he was still barely alive. Maverine wasn't a doctor and was unsure if a doctor could help a man like Tree if he could get him there on time.

Tree said softly. "Get me to the roof; it's still sunny outright?"

Maverine turned to see the sun setting, but it was still in the sky. He lifted the hulking tree man over his shoulder and made his way up the stairs. Kicking the service door leading to the roof off its hinges, Maverine immediately shut his eyes to ease the extremely agonizing pain, was able to get to the middle, and set his dying friend down.

Tree's bark hide began to absorb the sun's ultraviolet energy and slowly started to heal the fresh wounds. Tree patted Maverine on the back and gave him the go-ahead to go help the others.

So, determined to end this once and for all, Maverine recovered his goggles, retrieved his bag, and set out to do just that. He found the plans that the Chameleon had stolen for both locations and started to review each one, looking for his way in.

SUPERS: SPARKZ

The two ruthless bank robbers were impatiently sitting in Peterson's office. But not at the old Chronos building like before, this was located at another compound. For an office, it had no windows, a cement floor with an area rug that had three chairs and a cold metal desk resting on it. On the back wall, a large file cabinet. An odd office indeed, more like a bomb shelter hidden underground.

Peterson with two of his loyal clone bodyguards came in from behind; the agents stood guard at the doorway while their boss circled to have a seat in his dark leather chair.

"My dear apologies for my tardiness gentlemen; it's been a rather busy day." He reached for his fine oak cigar box and saw the discomfort glares coming from the one called Sparkz.

"It's been a while, hasn't it Stan?" Peterson stuck the Cuban between his teeth. As he bit the end and spat it out, he continued. "I've seen you've been up to the usual."

Stan was a renowned thief and has worked with some of the ones who are against Chronos which would make him a perfect asset. Stan was normal back in those days and didn't get his abilities until that day everything went wrong. When he felt the adrenaline surge through his body and shot that guard; it provoked the SBU outside to rush the building, shooting him and his other partner down. But when the paramedics used the defibrillator paddles to jump-start his heart; his powers manifested.

He spent the next few weeks in ICU until he was well enough to be sent to prison. Once he was able to figure out how to spark his powers, he honed them with practice by creating small arcs between his fingers. It wasn't until he stuck them too close to a socket that he discovered what he could truly do. The lights and power flickered throughout the building; as he charged his body with electricity, his wounds healed.

With two SBU agents stationed outside, they rushed in. After Stan struck them dead and cackled over their twitching bodies; he reached for the socket for more power. He then transformed into a being of pure electricity and shot into the wall. He followed the wires until they lead him to the power generator and caused a massive explosion.

With a sly grin, electricity surging in his eyes, Sparkz replied. "What can I say, with these new abilities, it makes robbing banks so much easier. And I must admit, with my dim-witted friend here, easier to fend off the Super buddies too."

Peterson nodded turning his attention to the partner and seemed almost impressed by him. Only a select few, like Sparkz and Peterson, knew this man's tremendous power. He was one to be most certainly feared. His strength matched some of the strongest Supers, was invulnerable and his third unique ability separated him from the rest.

If he spent the time to concentrate and focus his energies on a specific Super, he could temporarily hinder their abilities. He could even focus all his actions to blanket a small area and prevent any Super caught in that "dead zone" to lose their abilities. Of course, this leaves him vulnerable as well, as it too, shuts down his other two impressive powers.

"Awe yes Mister Borne. I've heard good things about you." The Negator wasn't much for words; he left the talking to the one with the brains. He nodded and thanked him, but left this conversation to the two of them.

Sparkz didn't want to waste more time; after all, time was money. They could be out there now preparing for the next heist. "So tell me, Mister Peterson, why did you send for us?"

The CEO of Chronos leaned back on his chair and explained. "I'm not sure how much the two of you follow up on current affairs," He paused as he looked the slower minded one up and down and figured at least one of them didn't and went on. "Let's condense it, shall we? There's a war on the brink and it's going to call upon every and all Supers in the city; they will need to choose aside. I'm offering you a spot on the winning team."

Sparkz scratched his messy blonde hair; he wasn't looking to join a group just to die. He knew the opponents he would most likely face if he were to agree but knew the kind of person sitting across from him. If he and his unique colleague were going to be "forced" to join, he/ they better be properly compensated for their troubles. And he knew, because of the man sitting next to him, how valuable they truly were.

"How much are we going to get paid if we join?"

With a shrewd grin, Peterson leaned in and responded. "Trust me, if this all goes well, you'll both be filthy rich; your little bank heist days will be a thing of the past."

The silent alarm was triggered; a red light rapidly began to blink in his office. The visiting two were confused as Peterson turned to his monitor on his desk. There on the screen was footage of the Junker and his team sneaking up on the underground facility.

With an alleviating smirk, Peterson replied. "Well, looks like you're going to be starting earlier than I thought. We have unexpected visitors approaching, deal with them."

Sparkz and his slow friend nodded and got up to get started as new mercenaries for Chronos. And some much-deserved payback for earlier.

Once gone, Agentman steps out from the dark corner to address his client. "Sir, I have just been informed by our sources on-site, that Venkman is making his way to the floating facility."

"Excellent. And you thought the subtle information we let Chameleon acquire wouldn't be enough.

"We are pleasantly disproven, Sir."

"Now I just hope that Bryan was able to retrieve Miss Marik's blood and a copy of the super being data will present itself soon. The pieces of my plan are finally coming together. Although we only have enough of her blood for the one procedure, it'll have to do for the time being. After it is done, we dispose of the subjects and leave town until things get settled."

"What about my promise?"

Peterson ignored the question and quickly scrounged up his important documents and made his way to the back of his office. There he kicked the bottom drawer of his wall-size file cabinet. When he did, it slid to the side, revealing a secret tunnel presumably leading to safety.

Before exiting, he said. "In due time my friend."

With his leather-bound pouch tucked securely under his arm, Peterson started down the tunnel when he noticed Agentman, his loyal henchman still standing in his office.

"Are you staying or coming along, I'm pressing the failsafe detonator in five?"

Agentman knew he was being deceived and bit his tongue. He began to call back all his clones in the immediate area. As they started to merge back, he followed his boss down the long dark tunnel as the door sealed shut behind them. After roughly ten seconds and a few dozen feet further into the tunnel, a series of small good places explosions were triggered that caused a cave-in, destroying all evidence of the escape tunnel.

Sparkz and the Negator navigated through the hallways while frantic scientists fled the scene. The alarms were silent, but in each room the lights flickered which signaled to those who knew, to flee. Up ahead, the band of heroes stepped out from around the corner and saw the bank nemeses approaching.

Glaring through his worn hockey mask, the Junker gave out commands. "Mal, take Kyle and go around and find his family, the lizard and I have some unfinished business with these two."

On separate sides of the narrow yet lengthy hallway, both parties exchanged glares. Sparkz was charging up his electricity for one powerful blast as the Junker and Chameleon drew their respective weapons.

Knowing they didn't stand a chance, the Chameleon muttered loud enough so only the man standing next to him could hear. "How are we going to do this? I mean he's just going to shut our powers down?"

The Junker grunted back. "How many explosives are you packing? I have a pound of C-4 on the bottom of my bag; for emergencies such as this."

"Ok, and then what; lure them down here and cave in the hallway?" The Chameleon double-checked the plan. "Will two pounds be enough?"

The Junker shared a chuckle as he replied. "Yours truly isn't the explosives expert, that's grumpy Mav's department." He slowly reached behind him, near the bottom of his golf bag, and added. "But the Junker's always game to try it out. When you're down by one point at the end of any game; you do the Hail Mary play."

Mal and Kyle went the long way around, searching for the prison location as indicated on the schematics stolen by their lizard friend. When they got to the area marked "cells" on the map, Kyle, who was standing behind Mal, pulled out a small blade.

"You chose the wrong side Mal." As the person changed their appearance so he no longer resembled Kyle. As he went to thrust the blade into Mallarian's back, a giant explosion from down the hall erupted, sending a shockwave of force their way which knocked both men forward, landing on their faces.

As both men slowly pulled themselves off the ground, Mal spun over on his back to confront the man who was about to backstab him. "I should have known you weren't Kyle, you just weren't charming enough."

"You're a fool and you won't be able to rescue them in time." The clone went to attack but was recalled back to the original Agentman before he got out of range. He completes the mission he was set out to do; ensure he tripped the surveillance if and when the group of heroes discovered the underground facility and give Peterson plenty of time to escape if need be.

Mal didn't waste time, he approached the metal slab cages and tried to look inside but it was pitch black. He tried calling out names, starting with; Pongo, Kyle, and then Brett but didn't get a response. He heard a slight growl followed by some faint panting but figured whoever inside just could be gagged.

Using his energy attack, Mal singed the lock off and as he pulled back on the handle to see who was inside, he found something else altogether. Out stepped from inside the prison on all fours, angry and searching for food, was a hulking mutated grizzly bear. This beast was massive; easily three times the normal size of its kind and aggravated by the mutation. It stood there for a moment and just drooled at Mal's presence.

The mutated bear suddenly lifted itself on its hind legs and unleashed a horrific growl.

Mal wasted no time as he stepped back and shot multiple blasts, each striking the chest of the bear and each just burning hair.

The bear hopped back to all fours and advanced to get closer to its prey.

Mal knew he didn't stand much of a chance in hand to hand with this hulking beast and since his energy blast wasn't affecting it, fleeing the other way was the next best option.

While on the run, Mal pulled out the schematics and gave it another glance to see if maybe they misread since they had a mole helping them before. Perhaps the captives were located someplace else down here.

The underground facility wasn't large. It was roughly a city block; 400 ft square, separated by rooms. It was Chronos' research lab more than anything else; this was where Mal, and others like him, were brought to be transformed into Supers. But it seemed Peterson's scientists were doing more than giving Normals and animals powers.

This was also where they created the negate serum and prototype artificial intelligent robots; it explains where the Hacker stole the schematics for his fake family. But up ahead and around the next juncture, on the map was indicated to be Peterson's office, and perhaps some answers.

With a blast of energy, the door blew off the wall and Mal rushed in to find it vacated. The remaining files that didn't go with the escapees, were now turned to ash; leaving no trace of evidence behind. Even now it wasn't marked on the plan, Mal knew there had to be a back door out of here for emergencies; how could there not be.

He saw the small indent in the file cabinet in the back of the office and went to investigate just as a cloud of dirty dust covered Junker and

Chameleon came running in and replaced the door, barracking it with the solid metal desk and anything not bolted down.

Mal kicked the bottom door and activated the sliding door of the cabinet, revealing a collapsed tunnel that presumably led out. There was no way any of them could dig out all that buried under a ton of rock and debris from above.

Defeated, Mal turned back and shared the depressing news. "Guys, we have to go back out that way. This one's sealed shut."

"Yeah, about the other way…" Junker paused to take a brief look back at what happened. He and the Chameleon went toe-to-toe but once they lost their powers to the Negator's unique ability, they tossed over their explosives and caved in the hallway on them. Since the Negator's power too was hindered, he was crushed under all that rock. There was no sign of Sparkz during all the chaos…

SUPERS: LOCK N LOAD

Growing up, Rob Lochart and Todd Logan were loners who loved reading and collecting comic books. Back when Supers first started to make a rise, they would rush to the scenes before, during, or after school to catch a glimpse. They told each other, "Someday when we get powers, we'll be the unstoppable duo!" They'd take turns daydreaming about when, not if, but when they get powers, what powers they'd have.

And on their sixteenth birthday, for Rob, that day finally came. He could fly, shoot energy, and create a personal field that absorbed damage. His buddy Todd hadn't got any powers, but that didn't stop the two from being the unstoppable duo. At night, Rob would come to his pal's bedroom window and fly him around the city, looking for crime.

Todd started to become skeptical about his lack of powers and that maybe he will remain a Normal. Their dreams of being that awesome duo would be crushed and with one being a Super and the other not, he worried it would part them.

But Rob said that would never happen, they would always be together like many heroes they'd admire in those comic books.

And on his seventeenth birthday, Todd finally got his wish. He could run extraordinarily fast and turn his skin into steel; making him both super tough and strong. Extremely excited, they started making their costumes to skip school and hit the streets.

Over the past week, they made several appearances to active crimes to put a stop to it. And when they showed up, after shouting their soon-to-be infamous catchphrase "Are you ready to Lock and Load!" They'd have to hear the criminals topple over laughing, their attempt at apprehending said criminals failed miserably.

They even tried to sign up to be a part of the City's Hero group and sauntered through the front door. There to talk to them was the infamous Junker; the rest were out on assignment.

The Junker always had his mask and gear on whenever he was in public; he was still keeping his identity a secret for the time being. "Isn't it a school day? Why aren't the two of you in class?"

Rob, since he was the first, was the leader of the duo. "We have spares. But never fear, we know you guys are short on heroes. So we're offering our awesome services." With that line delivered, both then struck commanding poses to help boost their chances.

The Junker couldn't help but let out a grin, good thing his mask covered it. He liked their enthusiasm, but they were nowhere near ready. "Listen, this is the majors, you guys just aren't old enough yet. Stick to the juniors, eat your vitamins, and come back in a few years."

With that rejection, it didn't crush their dreams, just prolonged them. Todd got the idea that since they weren't being taken seriously, they had to prove themselves. Once they thwart a few evil Supers diabolical schemes and outshined the heroes, they'd have no choice but to acknowledge their greatness.

But they did more harm than good, because of them interfering on several different occasions, both Lock N Load fumbled and stumbled, knocking over the veteran hero and allowing the criminals to get away.

Lock and Load were stalking the neighboring roof to the Heroes HQ, keeping an eye on what they were doing and if they could, follow them to the possible crime scene. It was getting rather dark out and they had to be home soon or face their parent's wrath. Just as they were about to call it a night, the notorious Maverine jumped from the platform down onto the same roof as them.

After landing hard and indenting the cement roof, Maverine went to continue to the next. But the young duo instantly recognized him and cut off his path.

Hovering overhead with his fists pressed against his hips, Rob commanded. "Halt Maverine, we are the dynamic duo, Lock, and Load, here to arrest you."

Todd added, with both fists held out in a boxer's stance. "Yeah, there's no room out here for criminals like you."

But Maverine didn't have the time to deal with these two jokers. So he did his best to ignore them and power his way through. "Listen, boys, it's getting dark out. Get home before the streetlights come on. I swear, I'm out doing well today."

The words of a known criminal usually meant nothing, that's why Lock N Load didn't oblige. They moved closer together and blocked the man's path. Maverine stopped and set his bag down. If they could see the fury in his eyes, they'd surely wet themselves.

Todd then asked. "Then why does it look like you're fleeing from the Heroes HQ?"

Maverine took a deep breath, he didn't want to harm these guys, but if it came down to it, if it meant getting to his friends in time, he'd certainly subdue them. But then he got thinking; take one from his brother's book. He was about to go in alone, back up would be nice;

or a good strong diversion at the least. Maverine found himself for the first time, about to admit he needed help.

With a grin signaling, 'I hate being proven wrong' he looked these guys dead in the eyes and asked for their help. He explained the seriousness of the situation and everything that's been happening. And, just maybe, if things all go well, Venkman would enlist them as heroes, but when they finished school of course. He'd at least suggest the idea.

This was the chance Lock and Load had always been searching for. Even though he was a notorious angry Super, an offer like that doesn't come across the table too often. So, after they exchanged giddy looks with one another, they came to a verdict. Overjoyed with excitement, they agreed.

Maverine led them back to where it all started; the thought to be abandoned, Chronos building. Maverine had a hunch since the underground facility wasn't too far from this building, Peterson would have an escape tunnel that would lead him back to the weapons floor, many sublevels under the main building.

He had Lock fly above and watch the rooftops while he had the speedster run around the back to keep an eye out. Maverine set his bag down and had out his personal favorite; a gigantic anti-tank cannon and rested it on his shoulder. He was positioned at the front, across in an alleyway.

And his suspicions didn't let him down. Calmly walking out the front door was a whistling Peterson with his personal bodyguard to his side, keeping a cautious eye for any surprises. Peterson was making his way to an unmarked van parked half a street down from the building.

Maverine slowly aimed the big cannon at his target and fired before Peterson stepped inside. The van exploded, knocking both victims back landing hardback in front of the Chronos building. Maverine swung the duffle bag over his shoulder and stepped out from the alley while reloading.

"You've been a bad man Peterson. I should have let you get in the van first, but Venkman wouldn't like that." He kept the barrel aiming at his prone foes. It wasn't long that both Lock and Load joined his side. The kids were thrilled, cheering the Maverine on.

Pulling out from his pocket, Peterson revealed the detonator. "If I press this button, you can kiss your friends in my underground facility goodbye."

With a cunning smirk, Maverine replied. "Come on Charles, you're defeated here. You don't have the data; you don't have your equipment or the data. Soon Venkman and the others will have the prisoners and you'll have nothing. So why don't we call it quits; it's getting late for these two."

Peterson savored the moment like he was waiting for something. He didn't appear to be disgruntled about being at the end of Maverine's barrel. "If that's what you think. Or perhaps I have everything I need and have everyone where I want them. Did you ever think of that? Did you ever think that this was all part of my scheme? Maybe Mallarian has been working for me this entire time?"

Maverine couldn't and wouldn't believe it. "You mean the guy who botched all his missions?"

With a crafty irritable grin, Peterson responded, "Did he now? Or did he fool you all into thinking that? I knew Kyle was working for Pongo and even with his family as leverage; he'd do the right thing. I knew you were a mole working for your brother. Even under all your noses, I managed to succeed. As for Mallarian, after he retrieved the data from Gadgetman, we had him tell Kyle he failed and personally handed it over to me. And I had him keep the facade going to distract you all while I set things into motion."

Maverine lowered his weapon, he couldn't believe it. "No, it's not possible."

"You're right, it isn't. We made that all up. We did it to buy the client time..."

That raised Mav's eyebrow, "Shit, you're not Peterson..."

It wasn't, just Agentman once again, pretending to be someone he wasn't. But the detonator in his hand was very real and pressed down on the button as he changed back to his old self. He was expecting a rather large explosion from down the road but got nothing. Behind them was the quirky scientist known as Q.

"I heard everything you said, you imposter. I'm jamming the frequency so you cannot detonate." Q then tossed a smoke grenade at the two clones and the green mist inside came shooting out. The clones went to laugh because they knew the negate gas did not affect them. However, it made for a great distraction.

Maverine and Lock aimed and didn't waste the chance.`

Both clones went down, one with a singed hole from Lock's blast, the other with a huge gaping hole where his chest used to be. Maverine nodded at Q to thank him.

Q informed him, "I got my guys drilling the debris from the tunnel to your friends. I'm glad you called..." The old man went back into the building and came back out with what looked like a new and improved set of goggles.

"Thanks, Q. I'm sure they'll come in use." He took the goggles and tucked them into his bag for now and asked. "So where'd that prick get off to?"

"Not a problem, as long as you stop breaking everything the Maverine touches." Q scratched his head to recall. "Oh, after your urgent call, he came in through the hole and took one of the proto-type helicopters I've been meaning to work on."

"Great, can you track it?"

"Why of course I can. We place trackers into everything we make. It makes it easier for the hired help to know where to recover them in cases like yourself; destroyed them beyond working condition." Q walked back towards the building with Maverine next to him. "I still don't understand how you malfunctioned that armored van, it's meant to ram into things... and yet, you did a number on it. It's still inoperable." Q continued to ramble on about nonsense, veering off track to the question asked.

Maverine was short on patience and cut in. "Q, can you track the helicopter?"

"Hold onto your goggles, I know where he's going. Peterson told that agent of his, he had to stop by the flying fortress for the rest of his plan. I don't know what he means, but I can tell you how long it took us to build those ion engines that keep the base suspended in the air. And do you know what it uses for fuel?"

Maverine didn't care for the technical details or want to waste the time to hear. He turned his attention to the kid who could fly. "You think you can get us all in the air?" Lock nodded and Maverine spun back to talk to a bumbling Q. "When you dig out the others, tell the Junker where we went. And just in case he wasn't lying, keep Mallarian out of the loop."

SUPERS: SERPENT STINGER

Stalking the night skies, desperately searching for its next Super victim to quench his hunger, the Serpent monster is what any Super should fear. But the beast has only been spotted after the sun goes down, never during the day...

That's because the Stinger unwillingly transforms each day; into the Serpent Stinger at dusk, and back to a homeless bum by day. The poor sap stuck with this unwanted curse has no recollection of the previous night's activities. He wakes up in a daze, assuming he spent it drunk as a skunk unaware of the evil deeds he committed that night.

And just as dusk began to settle in, the poor homeless man dropped to the ground and screamed out in sheer agony as his body began to tremble. During this horrific and excruciating change, his bones snapped to realign as his muscles tore; the transformation took several minutes until it was complete. And when it did, standing there in the small alley was a massive serpent creature; almost twenty feet in length, long deadly stinger tail, giant leathery wings, and a vicious snout.

After a long shrieking cry, the Serpent used its long razor-sharp claws to scale the wall and take to the air, practically drooling as it anticipated how delicious its next Super victim will taste.

Over the new week, the Serpent Stinger had faced and devoured roughly a dozen Supers, heroes, villains, or just other frightened ones. It didn't matter, they all tasted scrumptious. The first two just so happened to be criminals. Which explains why at first, the people saw him as a hero. But the next night, when an unnamed vigilante was saving a damsel in distress, the Serpent swooped down and ate him whole.

That was its first contact with the Super Heroes of the city; the White Light came to the rescue but was no match for the tough hide and incredible power this beast had to offer. But it remembers the Light, seeing it fly around in the air every night like a beacon. But as fast as this Serpent may be, it can't catch the speed of the Light.

But this night seemed different, the sun finally set, the beast was unleashed and took to the early night. Since last night, the Serpent didn't get any food; it would make up for it by eating two, perhaps three Supers. As it began the usual route, off in the distance it saw the shiny Light man heading straight for him. The Serpent couldn't help but crack a sharp toothy grin.

The Light stopped about a hundred paces out and fired a few light beams, making sure he had the Serpents complete attention.

And he sure did, even without shooting it. "Come on, it's lunchtime." The Light slowly began to fly away.

The Serpent didn't second guess and the chase started.

The Serpent kept pace with the Light, who was not flying at full speed. He was making sure he was able to lure it to where he wanted to go. High above the city, the Light headed for the only cloud in the night sky.

The Light led the beast straight into the cloud and beyond. The Serpent was dead set on getting his prey and not allowing him to escape his painfully hungry belly. Flapping its wings as hard as Super-ly possible, the Serpent ripped through the cloud. Once it broke through, it saw a massive floating fortress with Venkman, encased in his telekinetic force field, suspended in the air, fending off the Kid's super blast.

The Serpent paused, slowly its ascent, and gazed upon the buffet of Supers now at its disposal. It admired the Light for its generosity as it licked its snout, looking for a patsy that wasn't paying attention.

When the Light noticed that the Serpent followed his plan, he grinned and joined the battle. The Serpent was eyeing the hulking Bat as he was about to leap up and attack Venkman from behind. As the bat made the motion to move, the Serpent plunged and made its attack.

But the Bat didn't go without a fight, he saw the beast charge and turned just in time to snatch his snout and prevented himself from being devoured whole. But the tremendous strength of the Serpent was far past his own as he slid backward with the beast in tow.

The poisonous tipped tail of the Serpent shot around, striking the Bat in the ribs. The venom quickly went to work, weakening Superbat who then lost his energy and went limp, allowing the Serpent to feast. Happy but nowhere near satisfied the Serpent leaped back to the air just as the helicopter with Peterson and his loyal henchman arrived.

Surprised by a massive beast jumping from out of nowhere, Agentman tried to maneuver the helicopter but couldn't as they collided into the side and had to make an emergency crash landing. The Serpent was knocked out of the air and fell on top of the Kid.

Venkman landed next to it, placed his hand on the beat's forehead, and spoke softly the words, "Sleep peacefully." And just like that, the beast's eyes shut and went into a deep slumber.

Meanwhile, the Light blasted his way through the doors and blinded any guards stationed inside. But the hallway was vacant, so he continued down the hall, looking for the cells.

A restless Pongo came to and found himself on a small cot in a cell next to who he assumed was Kyle, but his face was covered with a black mask and was bound. Pongo tried to recall what happened and remembered his ring. He frantically searched every pocket but couldn't find his father's heirloom. Through the bars, he spotted it resting on the table across the way.

The Light blasted the outer door down and charged in. There were only Pongo and the masked man present inside the cells, no guards. It was rather odd, there were no guards so far anywhere on this flying vessel. After blasting the locks of the cells and opening the doors, Pongo retrieved his father's ring as the Light unbound Kyle's restraints and removed the hood.

"Come on, Venkman's holding them off outside, let's get out of here." The Light explained.

Kyle scanned the room and saw it empty. There was no sign of his family and knew by the layout exactly where he was. "Damn that Peterson..." As he was about to explain that there must still be another secret location, he received a text. When Kyle checked it, there was a photo of his wife and child bound in tears, with a mysterious dark figured standing next to them with today's date. Seconds later he got another text saying; it's time to do your thing.

Both rather curious, the Light and Pongo came to see what was on the text. But Kyle stuffed it back inside his pocket and said. "Guys, I'm sorry but I have to get them back." His overwhelming charm kicked in as he told them. "Now lock yourselves inside those cells."

They didn't argue and like mindless zombies, both walked inside the cells. As the doors locked, Kyle stuck his hand through the bars and requested from Pongo his ring. Against his will, Pongo didn't hesitate or second guess the request.

Kyle slipped the ring on as he left the room and met up with Venkman and the sleeping serpent just when Maverine, with Lock and Load, landed.

Peterson and his loyal henchman barely escaped the wreck and made it to the shadows, but knew if Kyle wasn't going to cooperate, it was only a matter of minutes before they were discovered.

Before the others could ask Kyle where the others were, the charmer marched up next to the leader of the heroes and told him. "Venkman, place a protective field around me." And without even thinking, he obliged. "Now turn towards those three and paralyze them."

As Maverine reached for his bag to react, Venkman held out his hand and used his psychic ability to temporarily shut down the nervous system of their bodies. But only Lock and Load were affected, Maverine drew his shotgun and aimed.

Kyle's eyes widened, he couldn't understand why as he ordered Venkman to do it again.

Since his brother was in a charm trance, Maverine explained. "Sorry bud, but I'm kind of immune to some of my brother's abilities." He stepped closer, keeping the gun trained on Kyle.

A giddy Peterson stepped out of the shadows clapping his hands. "Excellent work indeed gentlemen. Now will you finish this Kyle, we have to leave, the SBU are on their way."

Kyle hesitated, he knew what he had to do. But this wasn't the way to get his family back. Just as he was about to let his charm on Venkman go, Billy, the Kid walked through the sleeping Serpent and expelled his energy attack, striking Maverine in the chest. The blast wasn't enough to kill the super-tough target but did have enough force behind it to knock him back. Caught completely flatfooted, Mav lost his bag and flew over the edge.

Overwhelmed with the satisfaction of getting the drop on the infamous Maverine, the Kid couldn't help but gloat. "Did you see me pwn that douche bag?"

Kyle didn't seem impressed and stated. "You do know he'll survive that right? You only pissed him off."

But Billy didn't seem frightened, although he should have been. Instead, he shrugged and started to blast away at the Serpents belly, creating a huge hole. Seconds later, Superbat to come bursting out, gasping for air.

Billy mentioned. "That's another one you owe me Batty."

Superbat nodded, he didn't like the fact that this kid kept saving his life. But he was a professional and had some honor so he thanked him and joined his client's side.

The rest gathered around as Kyle charmed Venkman to tell Peterson where Sue took the boy. When Venkman didn't respond, Kyle tried again and still got no answer. Kyle couldn't explain it, after all, no one has ever resisted his charm, perhaps Venkman just didn't know.

Peterson wasn't irritated, he knew it was just another hill they were going to have to climb in this long journey. "Take him with us, we got some of the things we wanted to accomplish."

SUPERS: SBU

The Super Being Until is a secret branch of the joining governments who secretly investigate any and all things unexplainable. It started when the first Super was discovered and instead of being frightened and apprehensive, one man saw an opportunity. He suggested that the two of them find others like him and help them cope with their abilities. His vision was to unite and have Supers and Normals work together for the common goal; peace. They would pair a Super with a normal agent.

Some teams, like Agent Derrick Pongo; who was known to be affiliated with the notorious Maverine and the Wolf. Worked well and together and completed some of the most dangerous missions to date.

But most duos had a biased hatred each for the other. One was envious of the other while the other wondered why they were babysitting. It got so out of hand that, "Accidents" seemed to be happening more frequently for no reason. When the new Director took over, he banned Supers from being a part of the SBU.

So after almost a century of secrecy, the SBU is now a public figure. Normal people policing Supers and protecting everyone from criminals. A daunting task since they don't have impressive powers.

But all is not hopeless and thanks to brilliant people like Doctor Wynona W. Wells, the battlefield has been balanced out. She was able to create the serum all Supers fear. Something that negates the very thing you take for granted isn't usually well received by the recipient. And because

Supers rely heavily on their powers, they don't train their normal fighting skills like agents with the SBU do.

And once captured, a Super is escorted to an Island that "temporarily" hosts them until trial to see if they are deemed fit for civilization. But as of recent, the SBU feels all Supers, since 95% of them appear hostile, should be brought here for the trial. To this date, no Super has returned.

The SBU decided, on their own, to imprison each one and not give them the better of the doubt; orders from the new Director and his number one agent, Eric Pongo. They wanted permission to rule the Super community for their "own good". Neither trust Supers for their own personal reasons and that rage is what motives them each day.

But then the public rallied a petition, pleading for any Super to form a hero group to protect the citizens. After an embarrassing debate, the irritable Agent Eric Pongo, along with SBU Director Carey, saw it as an opportunity to get their special, Super registration act, to pass.

Their plan was simple, have this so-called hero group fail miserably and cause so much destruction, forcing the government's hand. Pongo knew it was just a matter of time for the cocky arrogant nature of the Supers to shine. But it wasn't happening fast enough for them.

What made matters worse was when the Chameleon was finally able to report back. He had no problem offering all information on what happened to him inside Chronos. Except for the Super change. He knew the SBU protocol.

Director Carey was so intrigued with this newfound idea of granting normal beings superpowers, he made it Pongo's number one priority to get it.

So Agent Pongo has been desperately trying to get some men back in there and getting a copy of that data. He saw this as a good way to kill two birds with one stone.

As the sun was setting, down by the docks that lead to SBU island, a dozen SBU agents were escorting a bound and hooded Ami Marik. They had an IV machine pumping that special serum into her veins, negating her power. It wasn't confirmed what abilities she truly possessed and they didn't want to find out the hard way.

They were hoping with all the "Super" issues popping up, the attack on her building, and now her sudden disappearance, her influence would eventually fade and they will get the needed votes in her absence.

They were just waiting to board the boat that brought them to the dreaded Island to arrive. It was mysteriously running behind.

Pongo's inside man Bill was on the scene and just received word from another agent on the events quickly unfolding near City Hall, home of the Heroes. "Sir, people are frantic, some are beginning to flee to their cars. There's an all-out war battling in the clouds above."

All the SBU on the scene turned to the single cloud floating high above their beloved city. Bright lights flashing and bursts of energy could be seen. Then they saw the hulking Serpent beast follow the White Light through the cloud. Did the City's Heroes need assistance?

Bill, who's had one crazy long day, began barking out orders. "Ok, we're going to need to get a few choppers up there. Agent Sterns, you take a small group and escort this Super to the island for booking; on the double."

The SBU helicopter quickly made its way up towards the floating vessel. When they were within range, Peterson ordered Kyle to use Venkman and bring the copter down. Just as the agents got within range to see who it was standing on the platform, the pilots went comatose, lost all control and the helicopter began to spiral down towards the ground.

After crashing through the roof and many stories of the City Heroes headquarters, a raging Maverine stepped out onto the platform just in time to see the helicopter barrelling down. With haste, he ran to the edge and dove at the right time to get inside the falling copter. Shoving the pilot out of his seat, Mav was able to take the stick and regain the controls just as it came to the ground; landing safely.

Now since they were far enough away from Venkman's control, the SBU agents suddenly came too. Each quickly drew their special weapon and aimed the notorious Maverine, even though he had just saved their lives.

With his hands in the air, Maverine knew he didn't have to, but wanted to explain. "Are you guys on some serious crack? I just saved your hides."

Bill stepped out front and replied. "Yeah, well we wouldn't have needed it if your brother didn't use his abilities on us. Now he's just bumped you down and took over number one. But I guess the SBU should thank him, after all, because of everything that's happened today you can bet the court is going to pass the Supers registration bill. Now we'll get to track you all down, legally."

"It's not him..." Maverine paused, it was going to take too long to explain and these guys didn't seem like they really cared. Plus it wouldn't help his cause anyway. He tried another approach. One he learned from his days working for the people aiming their guns at him. "Listen, let me go handle it and I swear I'll turn myself in once the smoke settles." Mav then extended his hand to shake on the pending proposal he gave.

Bill went to accept but paused. After all, he did remember a time when this man did work for the SBU, even though he wasn't an agent then. "Why should I trust you?"

Mav was blunt. "Because of the simple fact that I'm still here and am willing to negotiate?"

Bill nodded, after all the man was right and shook his hand.

"We'll be expecting to hear from you soon; trust me."

With a sly grin, Maverine bit his tongue and added. "Just one small favor. I'm going to need a ride back up to get my bag back."

When Maverine was gone, Bill made a call.

●　●　●

Bryan could run so fast, to everyone in his path, he was just a swift blur. He enjoyed it so much that he would deliberately gust up wind to lift skirts, knock off hats, and causing unaware victims to spill their coffees.

Bryan, as did every Super who wasn't already a resident on SBU Island knew one thing; don't stop to talk to an agent. Bryan ran as fast as he could, reaching up to 1000 kph, hoping to avoid unnecessary contact with the SBU and just snatch his target.

And there she was. At the dock with several armed agents. Bryan cracked a grin; he couldn't believe it was going to be this easy. As he whizzed past, he was able to snatch up, toss her over his shoulder and be around the corner a block away before anybody realized what happened.

And he wasn't a fool, he slowed down to a complete stop to ensure this was the captive he came for. He didn't want to get back to Chronos disappointed.

When he unveiled the prisoner, it wasn't who he thought, but a redheaded imposter who wasn't bound at all.

"You're so predictable, silly speedster." And then she jabbed the syringe she was palming into his chest and injected the serum to negate his abilities.

When her backup finally caught up, Agent Lena barked out. "Director Carey was right. She is a major part of this somehow. Escort her to the holding cell until we fully know why."

As the handcuffed the powerless Bryan, the agent holding him asked. "And what about this one?"

"Get what info you can get out of him and take him to the island." Lena pulled out her phone. "I need to contact my inside man and update him on what we've unraveled."

SUPERS: VENKMAN

From their birth to that one day, the twin boys of Brent and Cyndi were inseparable. They shared the same room that they ended up turning into a fort. Like most kids their age in this day and age, they would dream that one day, they'd be Super Heroes, just like in comics, and fight evil.

They say with twins, they have a connection to one another and these two were no different. it didn't matter where they were, far or near, they always seemed to know where the other was or even if the other was angry or scared.

And even though they were still Normals, they gave each other their Super nicknames. Venkman because he was sassy, sarcastic, and witty, but a born leader. Able to quickly process and control the situation by keeping a cool head. The other was Maverine, because he preferred to work alone and found his tactics sometimes a tad unorthodox. He thrived on getting into the action and getting his hands dirty.

But whether it be conquering the playground at recess, the snowbanks in winter, everyone wanted to be on the twins' team. Until that day came.

It was the boys' tenth birthday when it happened. As they blew out the candles and like each year, wished for cool abilities, but for only the one, it finally came true.

That was the day little Venky discovered his potential. At first, he was able to read the surface thoughts of others but as time went on, his powers grew stronger and the more he gained.

It didn't take long for their parents to figure it out and when they did, they weren't afraid, or angry but proud. Proud because they knew the kind of son they brought up and knew he would use his abilities for good.

But over time, while praising Venkman and his powers, Maverine became the shadow, no longer the equal. He hadn't received his special gifts and after many years of waiting, all he saw was his brother get stronger.

At the age of sixteen, a jealous Maverine ran away, far from his brother's telepathic reach. Venkman knew the reasons for why he left and felt that maybe for now; they should part. Well at least until his brother could come to terms with it. Besides, he found it somewhat weird that he couldn't exactly pinpoint which direction he went. It was like he was in two spots at once.

But it wasn't until almost a decade later when they reunited. But who Venkman managed to track down wasn't his brother per se. It was the reason why earlier he had troubles tracking him. The old grizzled man he found was his brother, but much older. There had been two of them all along.

This Maverine explained the reasons why he left and apologized for them. Without giving too much of the future away, he explained how he was always watching the two of them, and ensuring their safety, but kept a distance.

So Maverine did get his powers that day as well. But his weren't visible at first. Whenever something doesn't kill Mav, he gets stronger and tougher. And because of his amazing regeneration, he healed things that could kill him. A minor cut would increase his power. But over the years, he discovered that his sensitivity to light, also increased.

Their powers were abnormal because usually once a Super receives their abilities, they stay the same for their entire lives, never increasing.

Perhaps why Peterson wanted Venkman over poor Brett all along.

When Pongo first came to Venkman with his suspicions on Chronos' secrets, he knew the politics and red tape would stop him. So he decided to ask his older brother, who's already an outsider, to pose as a mercenary.

Maverine figured this was the fork in the road that would ultimately alter the future and agreed to help, hoping, since this time, he was a Super, he could make it better.

This brings us to where we are now.

In yet another similar secluded office at another undisclosed Chronos facility, a charmed Venkman was still like a rock in his chair with Dr. Wesley Wells ejecting his blood. There was no point pumping the negate gas because it was well known, it did not affect psychics. Plus it wasn't needed since Kyle never left his side.

Venkman was still aware inside his own mind of what was happening outside. He just had no control over his actions. He tried to fight the charm bestowed onto him, but he was no match. He wasn't too worried, because he knew his brother would be able to find them and wouldn't give up until he did.

And since all day, nothing was going according to plan, so The Kid, Superbat, and multiple Agentman clones were stationed outside. They had one simple task, make sure there are no interruptions during this very important procedure. Agentman was also standing next to his boss, giving him updates from other clone members when they rose.

An irritated Peterson was on the phone looking rather displeased with the poor sucker on the other end.

Peterson did his best to remain calm. "Ok, it seems the SBU have contained Bryan and Miss Marik. They are now on the island. Why are there all these pesky hitches in my plan? And the super being data, any news on that?"

Peterson nodded as he was informed by the techie on the line that he reviewed all footage of the surveillance in the building and on the elevator saw Mallarian tuck what looked like a disc into his special little pocket dimension before meeting up with Kyle earlier in the day. Peterson asked for the time of which it happened and hung up.

Shaking his head, Peterson sought the truth. "You've been keeping things from me, Kyle. Do you not remember the last time you tried to deceive me?"

Kyle didn't need to be reminded, it's why he's now only trying to save his wife and one child instead of two. He just sat there in silence allowing the man to continue.

"Mister Mallarian possesses a disc, a disc he obtained around the time he was sent to Ned Carvers home. Can you explain why he didn't hand it over? Are you losing your ability to control your power?"

Kyle didn't verbally reply, he just slightly turned to Venkman. He had full control, but couldn't answer why he let Mallarian loose. Not without angering the man in front of him.

Before the situation escalated for the worst, Agentman informed them. "We have word from one of our people who is keeping an eye on Q for you. They have managed to just break through the collapsed tunnel and are now recovering the Junker and Mallarian as we speak."

"Excellent, eliminate both of them immediately, recover the disc and have your agent bring it here on the double. We will have everything we need to move my procedure forward."

Kyle raised an eyebrow, after all, he thought one thing was still missing; the blood of Marik. And when he asked, Peterson erected the evilest smirk.

He also felt the need to boast and share. "I have a vial stashed away for me. I will be in need of more for my promises to Agentman here and further procedures for myself. But since I have Venkman here and under your control, I can get the powers I want now. And don't worry about your family, once this is all finished you can go to them. I will no longer need your services."

Kyle nodded and thanked the man.

Peterson then asked for him to take Venkman to the procedure room, leaving the two alone.

"Once Kyle completes this last task of his, take care of him and his family. I grow tired of his whining and lack of trust because after all, he's still and will continue to be a potential threat after this is all said and done."

"As you wish sir; will there be anything else before your operation?"

"Just ensure that we are not interrupted, but I believe that goes without saying." Peterson put his cigar out and rose from his chair.

He was so overwhelmed with glee he couldn't help but smile. He couldn't remember the last time he felt this good inside. He even commented.

"I can't believe this conniving plan is finally reaching its end. It almost brings a tear of joy to the eye, doesn't it?"

But the apprehensive Agentman still stressed their concerns. "Sir, are you certain with all these events unfolding, that this is the right thing to do at this time? Wouldn't it be better to wait until the heat is off of us?"

"Trust me, I would prefer to do this under different circumstances, but I believe I have waited long enough Mister Man. I do not wish to wait any further. Also, once I have Venkman's abilities, these tedious annoyances will be easier to handle, thus, making future endeavors that much easier. I will no longer need to rely on useless and whiney amateurs to get results."

Agentman and his clones nodded and spoke together. "As you wish Sir, but just one thing. How do we recover the data if the subject has it in his pocket dimension?"

Rubbing his chin, Peterson thought out loud. "Hmm, we're going to need his services once more."

SUPERS: Q

The Chameleon went back to blending in with the background just as the drill finally broke through. Several curious scientists inched their way through the unsettled debris and found both Mallarian and Junker impatiently standing there Marching out the Junker muttered. "About time you dweebs dug us out. By the way, you might not want to go out into the hallway without packing some serious gear first. A wild Super bear is on the loose. Not to mention, those petty dumbasses your boss hired to try to take us down; are under a few tons of concrete. I'm not sure if the one survived."

Q was there to greet them back into his lab and was about to tell him what Maverine asked. "Is it just the two of you fellows in there?"

The Junker nodded; after all, he didn't want to give up their invisible friend. Mallarian had talked to Q before and asked. "What's going on now Q? What did we miss?"

Q remembered what his old buddy Mav said, and was apprehensive to speak, but needed to let the Junker know.

The City's Hero felt the hesitation, figured as to the reason, and gave him the go-ahead nod of approval.

"Lots is going on, that's what." Q turned back and escorted the two back inside his lab while blabbing on.

He veered off track and went back to his crazy old ways; mumbling incoherent rants about having to replace everything he's ever handed out. And how he's even carefully dictated that he wishes that every item borrowed are to be returned unscathed.

"Why don't they teach their people the word unscathed? Unharmed, not damaged, am I using the right term for you youngsters?"

With their patience growing thin, trying not to lose his temper, the Junker kept his cool and cut in. "Q please, we need to get out of here and back into the game. Our teammates are counting on us."

Mallarian stood there in silence. He was finally seeing the bigger picture unraveling before him. There was way more going on in the background than he thought. Everyone was not who they seemed to be, double agents working on the inside. Who could a man trust?

Q stopped and went back to being normal for a moment. "Maverine informed me of the situation; hence why we just spent the past hour digging the two of you out. He also told me to tell you that he will be at the flying fortress which is currently hovering over City Hall."

Q rounded the corner and entered his office. "That reminds me of a story; it was when we were building those damn engines that enable that massive beast to suspend over the city as it does."

Mal and the Junker had their next move and didn't want to hang around with the whacky man any longer than needed. So seeing that Q was just ranted on about nothing once again, they slipped out for the exit and into the elevator.

Already inside was a slender male scientist who pressed the button for the main lobby.

With their backs to him, both men remained quiet, not wanting to speak a word of their mission in front of any Chronos personnel.

But this was no ordinary tech geek. With their backs to him, this geek altered his appearance, changing back to who he once was. In each hand, he held a syringe with enough serum to render their powers useless for a long time.

As he slowly brought the needles closer to their necks, the Chameleon broke cover and kicked the items out of his hands.

Shocked, both Junker and Mal went to see what was going on, but the clone delivered two fast attacks, temporarily dazing the two while he dealt with the lizard. After receiving and dealing a few punches and kicks, it was clear, the clones fighting skills were not easily matched. After a roundhouse kick that brought the Chameleon to the ground, the Junker shook it off and got back into the game. About after a series of his punches were easily parried, he too was brought down when the clone kicked in his knee.

Mal spun around with his hand out, ready to blast but the clone wrapped his arm around and locked up his arm, redirecting the blast, forcing Mal to shoot the Junker in the chest. Mallarian continued to struggle with their assailant as the Chameleon leaped up and from behind and wrapped his arm around the clone's head. From the ground, the Junker reached for the syringe that was lying restless on the opposite side of the fight.

The clone smiled, he enjoyed a good fight as he jerked his head back and bringing his free leg up, simultaneously striking both attackers in the face. But he knew he was outnumbered and mentally contacted his original to send in backup.

About halfway between Q's lab and the main lobby, the elevator came to an abrupt halt. Momentarily confused Mal was about to ask just as the doors slid open and when they did, the clone engaged in the fight disappeared as well as the Chameleon. He moved equally as fast as he leaped up and exited the elevator cab.

Once the doors fully opened, the Junker found himself alone and staring down an open baseball field with multiple pitching machines hurling fastballs his way. The first dozen were direct hits to his chest and after dropping to a knee, he pulled out his trusty baseball bat and swung for each ball.

For Mallarian, the first thing he noticed as the doors open was Kyle, staring back at him. With his hand out, he politely asked. "Open your gateway and hand me the disc."

Mallarian tried to resist but found his hand moves without thinking. His arm rose as he unwillingly opened the portal. Crackling blue energy ripped through the air opening his portal which only he could see what was inside. A fair-sized closet full of random items such as his swords, guns, and on the floating desk sat the disc everyone has been looking for. He removed the disc and shut the gateway afterward.

Kyle couldn't hold back the satisfied grin. And when he stuck out his hand and accepted the disc from the frustrated Mallarian, he transformed back into the master of disguises, Agentman.

●　●　●

After the helicopter dropped Maverine off, he wasted no time to scour the area, only to find it vacant until he reached the cells. There he found two bewildered men trapped inside. After removing the cage doors with his super strength, he asked what happened. But he didn't need an answer, he already knew.

Pongo and the Light were no longer under Kyle's charm as they got interrogated by Maverine.

Completely ignoring the Light, Mav talked to just Pongo. "Are you up for what's going to happen next? It's going to get rough before it's over and trust me; it's going to be all over soon."

The Light felt hurt that he wasn't asked. "Hey, I'm up for it. Aren't you going to ask me?"

Maverine just glared and turned to walk away. He muttered from afar. "Come if you want a light bulb, just stay behind me."

He turned to see a smirk curl up on Pongo who saw the dumbfounded look through the mask.

He felt the need to clarify. "It's because you're too bright for him."

A bit confused, the Light remarked. "He's jealous of my smarts? I barely passed through the school. That can't be why you sure?"

Pongo shook his head and made it clear. "No, do you seriously not get it? He has light sensitivity. You literally expel a blinding light; even now you're probably causing him pain, even with those goggles."

The Light dimmed down and said. "He could have just asked me to put the light out, gees."

Maverine not only recovered his bag but found both Lock and Load recovering from being unconscious. He gathered everyone around in a circle to form a plan.

Pongo was about to share his suggestion when the speakers blared out Peterson's conniving voice.

"I see you're all still alive and on my property. Pity, I really liked that location, but you leave me no choice." With that message sent, from his office, Peterson pressed a button that cut the power to the engines.

With the fortress plummeting down to the Earth, the group began to panic as Mav did his best to assess a solution to the pending problem.

Sure, the Light and Lock could fly, but each could carry one other with them.

If Pongo had his ring, it wouldn't be an issue and when Maverine mentioned it, Pongo informed him that Kyle took it.

A troubled Tree looked up from the roof of City Hall. All he could do was watch the underside get larger and larger. He knew there wasn't time to flee, but he fumbled about to see what he could do.

Mav turned to both Lock and the Light and came up with a solution. "Ok, you each take one of those two and fly off. I'll stay here and figure something out."

There was no way any of these guys were going to leave one man to die.

Lock brought up. "Yo dude, there's no way we're bailing on you like that."

Maverine didn't have time to argue and knew he'd survive the crash. Or at least he hoped. He turned to the others. "You know I'll be fine, so get going."

The others didn't argue and said they'll meet him at the bottom.

Maverine looked ahead to see where the fortress would crash. It was heading down towards City Hall, so he leaped up and came stomping down, hoping his strength could set it off course. And it slightly had an effect. But it still grazed the side of the Heroes headquarters, causing much damage before colliding into the vacated park.

Tree just barely avoided the collision and fell through the gaping new of the wreck.

Maverine leaped off and landed on the platform where the others met up with him.

As they all gawked at the smoking wreck, the two youngsters commented. "Yo dudes, I hope this doesn't ruin our chances on getting in."

Maverine replied. "Don't worry about it junior; I'll take the full blame here. I always do. It's nothing new." As he stared down, he remembered. "Damn, I left my bag on that thing." And before the others could offer him a lift down, he jumped.

Pongo turned to the kids and said. "Listen, you two should be getting home. Leave this part to us."

Lock burst out laughing as he replied. "Are you kidding chief? This is just getting to the good part."

"Exactly, this is going to be dangerous; it's meant for the vets to get the job done."

Both youngsters took commanding poses and in unison replied. "We're ready to Lock and Load!"

The Light just shook his head to the terrible cheesy lines.

SUPERS: PETERSON PART 2

With his bag hung over his shoulder, Maverine with his brave posse marched down the street making their way to the entrance of the first Chronos building. Maverine could feel his brother's presence and let that guide him to Peterson. After blowing a hole with a grenade at the entrance, through the smoke they entered.

Patiently waiting to greet them was the Chameleon, who informed them exactly which level and how to get there. But after sharing the information, everyone but Maverine unexpectedly collapsed to the ground.

"Thank you brother, it allows the Maverine to venture in alone," Mav muttered as he made his way to the stairs.

He had no trouble finding the hidden level as he kicked the well-concealed door open and watched as he flew down the empty hallway. Quiet and subtlety weren't usually part of Maverine's strategies; there just wasn't time for such things. He did however like these new goggles Q gave him. They had different toggles; night vision, infrared, and thermo. So he knew exactly where to go.

He rounded the corner and saw through the huge observation window a secluded laboratory with a handful of scientists.

The main cast was present, including Doctor Wesley Wells who was overlooking the super procedure. Medik to ensure nobody died and

Agentman and all his clones for protection. Peterson was lying on one table while Venkman was tied and hooded with Kyle by his side across the room.

Fueled with rage, hate, determination to get this over with, Maverine made his approach. But before he got there, from the side, outrushed the Bat with his claws out ready to attack. In the struggle Maverine swung his bag around and struck his opponent in the head, knocking him off his feet.

While struggling to fend off the Bat, Maverine drew the pistol tucked down his pants and managed to fire off a few rounds at the glass. The window shattered and a stray bullet pierced through and struck Kyle in the left shoulder. As Kyle dropped from the hit and momentarily stunned, his charm over Venkman and everyone else was broken.

The very first thing Venkman did when he was free was to break his control over everyone.

Medik immediately rushed over and tended to Kyle's wound.

The innocents scrambled to flee as Agentman, along with his clones, surrounded their boss to ensure his safety.

Everyone was slow to get up from being mind paralyzed by Venkman. The Junker snapped out of their hallucination, almost striking Mallarian in the head, thinking he was a giant baseball.

Mallarian was able to regain full control over himself once more. Full well knowing what he was just forced to do.

Upstairs the Supers managed to get back to their feet and find their bearings as Billy the Kid came through the wall and immediately greeted them. Not wasting time with theatrics, the Kid started hurling his impressive energy bolts at the group.

The load was caught off guard as he took a blast to his chest and flew back smacking his head against the far wall.

Lock cried out as he and the Light retaliated with blasts of their respective elements.

During the firefight, Pongo snuck off to the side and made his way down the stairs with his special service sidearm in hand. With his free hand, he pulled out his phone and one thumbed texted his old friend inside the SBU; "bring every available agent to the smoldering Chronos building, I got all targets on-site."

Maverine and the Bat were entangled with one another, trying to oust the other by using their impressive strength. They were in a standstill and locked up, hoping the other would eventually slip up.

Meanwhile, Venkman used his psychic ability to force the squirming scientists to flee and never return. He took the hand of Doctor Wesley Wells and wiped the precious memories of the super being data so he would never remember.

Peterson slid off the table and snuck behind two Agentman clones as he rummaged to collect the disc and the ample vials of Super blood together and stashed them into a steel briefcase. He then searched for his emergency exit.

Meanwhile the clones drew their pistols and aimed the Maverine but didn't fire in case they accidentally hit their friendly. But Peterson didn't care and ordered them to shoot anyway.

When the clones hesitated to reply, Peterson became enraged and repeated the order, adding. "Do your damn job to ensure my safety."

The clones didn't obey again; instead turned around and holstered their weapons. The two clones snatched the briefcase from the puzzle grip of Peterson. Confused, Peterson demanded to know what they were thinking.

"We don't think you're going to keep your end of our promise. So we're taking it for ourselves and will find someone else." And with that said, the one tossed a flash grenade and when everyone could see again, they were long gone.

The Bat stopped struggling with Maverine once he heard Peterson give the go-ahead to shoot him. "I'm not going to fight you Mav, if you want him, he's all yours."

Mal and the Junker arrived just in time to corner the CEO of Chronos and prevent his inevitable escape.

Venkman stood next to Kyle and nodded; that nod was a sign that he understood what Kyle felt he had to do at the time. Kyle gave the, thank you nod in return.

Feeling the need to end it once and for all, Maverine pulled out his big caliber rifle he'd been itching to use on the man with a cigar for some time now. He was about to pull the trigger but suddenly stopped by his brother using his telekinetic power on him.

Explaining his action, Venkman said. "No Mav, this isn't the way."

"You're kidding me right now, right? He's just going to keep doing this until someone grows the balls to stop him." Maverine knew he wasn't going to win the argument and lowered his weapon. "I've killed him a few times before and he's still standing here. I don't know why."

Mallarian then thought, looking back over everything that's happened. The name of the company and with what Pongo told him. He explained it to the rest. "That's because his power is immortality. If you kill him, he'll just rise back up. Chronos; Father Time."

Maverine nodded, "Explains why he's like a bad penny."

Kyle raised his hand and asked. "Hey, before we decide on anything here, I just want him to answer my question; where's my family?"

The Bat, who transformed back to his human self, answered the pending questions of both Kyle and Medik. "I know where they all are. I'll take you to them after this."

Peterson seemed calm, after all, they were right; this wouldn't be the first time he's died. He will be back. Full of confidence and while they argued, he picked up his lit cigar from the ground and sucked in the intoxicating fumes. "Fools, when I do return, I will make sure you all pay dearly. Next time I won't be so considerate."

The Junker unclenched his fist to reveal the syringe he snagged from the elevator and Mal took it. But realized it was cracked and it was empty.

The tension was rising, but nobody knew what to do. Venkman went to read Peterson's mind. But he was a blank sheet. Not thinking one thing; he was too smart for that.

Unsure of what to do, behind the heroes a shot was fired. As everyone spun to see who took the shot, they saw a relieved Pongo holding his SBU service serum gun.

In unison, they turned back around to see a jaw-dropping surprised Peterson fall to his knees as he removed the dart embedded in his chest. The serum acted fast as it negated his powers and he began to rapidly age. His skin wrinkled and what little hair he had grew. Time was catching up to him, but he didn't die.

As everyone watched in horror, Mav stepped closer and aimed when he said. "Like I always say, if you want the job done right, use a bigger gun." And didn't hesitate or wait for someone to stop him. He squeezed back on the trigger.

The bullet ripped through the air and the chest of the CEO of Chronos.

Lying there in a pool of his own blood, the others gathered around to hear Peterson cough up the words. "So this is what dying truly feels like." He cracked a smile and added before fading off. "The hundredth time is the charm huh."

Everyone took a moment as the battle above still took place.

The Kid cackled as the blasts passes straight through his ghost-like body and did no harm to him. He returned fire, but the force bubble of Load absorbed the last hit before disappearing.

"Damn, he's brought my defense field down. This Kid's powerful."

"And annoying, he boasts more than I do." The Light remarked as the Kid charged up his next attack and then unleashed a blast that was twice as dangerous as his others. The blast managed to strike Load in the chest and brought him down.

Down below, Maverine explained the SBU and the bill had been passed. That also meant that temporarily the Heroes headquarters was shut down. He was unsure of Tree's fate but presumed he was being arrested and will most likely be escorted to the island.

"I already took the blame," He looked at his brother and added. "Take these guys and hit the basement. There Q can guide you through the tunnels, find some safety for now. No sense in all of us being captured. Hopefully, Ami can get our names cleared and everything will go back to normal."

Venkman went to argue, but deep down knew this was the best plan. He nodded and took the team of Supers down the elevator.

Mav grabbed his bag and headed up the stairs. There he found the Light barely dodging and fighting the Kid with the smoldering bodies of Lock and Load off to the side.

Maverine stepped between the two as he took one of the Kid's devastating blasts directly to his chest. He wasn't impressed, but it was enough to stop the other two from attacking. While his body healed the fresh wound, he warned them. "Listen, the SBU is going to be on us at any moment."

The Kid let out a wicked grin and replied. "Please, let those Normal dweebs come. I'll just blast them all down." He let loose a loud cackle before adding, "It'll be like shooting fish from a barrel. Like in Call of Duty, blast down the cannon fodder."

The Light shook his head; maybe this kid did deserve that fate for himself. "That won't solve anything. Sounds to me that Mav's plan is for you to go into hiding. Not for me though, I'm one of the City's infamous Heroes. I will be returning to the skies and being that beacon innocents turn to when the dark side of criminals cast over them."

Maverine cut in and shot him down. "Sorry bulb boy, but you can't go back neither. I'm positive they shut the hero unit down, especially after Venkman's stunt earlier. Just fly on outta here and as for you junior, why don't you be like a ghost and vanish."

As the Light zipped off, the Kid glared at the big man but didn't say or do anything about it. He then ran through the wall.

Moments passed by and Maverine stood in the middle of the vacant lobby, impatiently waiting for the arrival of the SBU.

SUPERS: MAVERINE PART 2

Maverine sat back and rested his hands behind his head. "Well, that pretty much sums it all up for you."

Doctor Greene was listening as she twirled her pen around between her fingers. "Uh-huh, I see and you aren't going to disclose the whereabouts of the missing Supers?"

"Sorry sweetheart, I'm not going to do the SBU legwork. You wanted a war with the Supers, you got one. I think you should just eliminate this whole silly registration bill before things get too far out of hand. But I am a man of my word, well today I am. So let's get this over with." Maverine stood up just as the SBU agents stormed Kyle's office inside the ruined Chronos building.

As they cuffed him and removed his goggles, they immediately replaced them with darkly tinted sunglasses. Now there were able to wrap this special mask that pumped the negate gas into his lungs. Now without his powers, the dark figure standing in the doorway stepped out of the shadow.

Grinning from ear to ear was Eric Pongo clapping. Back around his finger was his father's ring. "Excellent work indeed Maverine. You proved me... wrong."

Enraged, Maverine went to attack, but now powerless he couldn't shrug off the agents containing him.

Pongo felt the need to explain. "What can I say? I used you, I used Mallarian; heck, I used you all. But hey, Peterson was constructing one heck of a diabolical plan. So two birds with one stone right? Sure I had to work outside SBU protocols, resort to my father's tricks and rely on Supers to get the job done. But I knew, if I was able to get you involved and knowing your methods, you'd rain down destruction.

I had Gadgetman install a virus that not only wiped the data but upload false ones. One, in particular, the "plan" the Beginning had to turn on them.

All you Supers just focus on the threat before you. Not the one hiding under your noses. It's ok, you forced the government to pass the bill, and here we are. Simple and almost flawlessly executed I would say. Of course, I rather have had you all rounded up at the end and brought to the Island for safekeeping, but hunting you all down will be interesting in itself."

Maverine continued to struggle, but it did no good; he just couldn't overpower the numerous agents holding him.

Pongo continued to walk around the captive and unravel his plot. "Now, even though The Director wanted that super being data; I presume to take one from Peterson's handbook. Create super SBU agents, force, I mean have Kyle charm them into hunting down their fellow Supers. A project he dubbed; Project Chronos.

I'm personally thankfully we didn't. It means I can implement my idea instead. A most ingenious plan I must admit. Courteous of your old friend Q of course. A real genius inventor he and his late son were..."

A loud thump shook the entire floor. The vibrations carried throughout, startling the prisoner at first. The mechanic movements echoed throughout the hall. The continuous noise and vibrations of this mysterious figure carried on until it finally marched inward.

Standing in the doorway was a seven-foot hulking power-armored bodysuit. Armed with the latest in Q branches technology. A massive energy cannon, a heads-up display similar to Maverine's new goggles, and possessed the ability to fly.

"There were two reasons why I was meeting up with Gadgetman today. Even though he was murdered, we were able to recover data from the damaged computer from his warehouse. As you can see, the schematics we were able to find are quite impressive. Plus we were able to locate these twelve prototype suits in the sublevel of that warehouse."

Doctor Greene grew impatient. "Enough boasting, get this dangerous Super to the Island and find his colleagues before they escape and get out of the city."

But Pongo wanted to savor this moment; after all, he'd been looking forward to it for some time now. "I have a man keeping an eye on them. I think Mister Maverine here wants to know why. He and the recently deceased Wolf were responsible for the death of my father. While trying to help Supers and figure out why Peterson was collecting them, my family gets murdered. I despise all Supers; they brought the world nothing but greed and death." He took a long sigh, he finally got his true feelings off of his chest. "Now you can take him away. We have more to track down."

He watched with a satisfying grin as his agents forcefully removed the prisoner from his sight. Pongo turned to the gaping hole, in deep thought as he twirled his ring. He observed the dark skies above. Flying around, stalking the streets, in search of any Supers, were numerous amounts of these power suits. They spotted one Super and took action. The poor Super was no match and was easily subdued.

Pongo erected a most wicked grin. His plan was flawless. He remarked. "That's right, nowhere is safe, the SBU will find every last one of you. It's only a matter of time. And so the war begins..."

THE END